Judas *and* Jezabel

Judas and Jezabel
The Tales Of A New York Nanny

C.Y. Brown

Copyright © 2016 by C.Y. Brown.

Library of Congress Control Number: 2016910384
ISBN:	Hardcover	978-1-5245-1267-5
	Softcover	978-1-5245-1266-8
	eBook	978-1-5245-1265-1

All rights reserved. No part of this book may be reproduced or transmitted in any form or by any means, electronic or mechanical, including photocopying, recording, or by any information storage and retrieval system, without permission in writing from the copyright owner.

This is a work of fiction. Names, characters, places and incidents either are the product of the author's imagination or are used fictitiously, and any resemblance to any actual persons, living or dead, events, or locales is entirely coincidental.

Any people depicted in stock imagery provided by Thinkstock are models, and such images are being used for illustrative purposes only. Certain stock imagery © Thinkstock.

Print information available on the last page

Rev. date: 06/24/2016

To order additional copies of this book, contact:
Xlibris
1-888-795-4274
www.Xlibris.com
Orders@Xlibris.com
743725

Contents

Introduction vii
Prologue ix
Chapter 1   Getting Acquainted 1
Chapter 2   Secrets and Treachery 6
Chapter 3   Motherhood 11
Chapter 4   Carol's Realization 17
Chapter 5   Mind Games 23
Chapter 6   Betrayal 27
Chapter 7   Connor's Confession 31
Chapter 8   Seductive and Clever 34
Chapter 9   House of Horrors 38
Chapter 10   Walking on Eggshells 43
Chapter 11   Trouble and Confusion 46
Chapter 12   The Root of All Evil 50
Chapter 13   Trust 55
Chapter 14   Lies and Deception 59
Chapter 15   Trying Times 62
Chapter 16   Deceived 65
Chapter 17   Intervention 69
Chapter 18   Sacrifice 72
Chapter 19   Lawsuit 74
Chapter 20   Tense Moments 76
Chapter 21   Carol Now 80
Chapter 22   Lawsuits 85
Chapter 23   The Settlement 88

INTRODUCTION

This book is an extension of my views and opinions of our society in modern day. We, as people, have become materialistic, greedy, and lustful for all things that glitter like gold. It is our downfall to sacrifice love, inner peace, and harmony for the riches and spoils of the flesh. As a woman who is Americanized and who has adopted many of the strong American values, I, too, have seen a flaw of that specific value.

Every woman wants the perfect man—a strong man, a family oriented man, and a man with a decent to good bank account. But when does one cross the line to sacrifice love, harmony, and family for the greed of riches? One has truly sold her or himself to the house of selfishness, lies, and betrayal.

If we don't live in the path of righteousness and love, our morals as a people will not only fail ourselves and our culture but the adults of tomorrow—our beautiful children.

Disclaimer: This book is a work of fiction. Names, characters, businesses, places, events and incidents are either the products of the author's imagination or used in a fictitious manner. Any resemblance to actual persons, living or dead, or actual events is purely coincidental

PROLOGUE

I write this book to all my male relatives because the same way that there are men who prey on women, women too can be just as devious, seductive, and users in one breath. I want them to be aware of the Judas and Jezebels of the world so that they don't fall into the traps of evil and materialistic people. I write this book to open their minds and also to give someone a little food for thought. Hopefully, my words will not be ignored, and someone can save themselves from being trapped.

I can talk about the wonderful experiences I had in the past with previous rich and famous employers, but I prefer to cut to the chase and spare the details because they are not important to the story I want to tell. However, I will mention that I worked for some well-known people such as, the prince and princess of Saudi Arabia, a senator's daughter, a movie producer's daughter, an African-American comedian/actor and movie producer, a Supreme Court judge, and as well as doctors, lawyers, and a CEO and president of a large pharmaceutical advertising company. They all treated me well. I guess my background and experience helped gain the respect from these highly educated people. Never in my wildest dreams did I imagine I would come across a Looney-Toon employer that would end my career with such a bad taste in my mouth. There are a lot of people who are undiagnosed with mental illnesses, and we tend to ignore the signs. Hats off to P.H. Ds. Thank God I'm a strong minded person. Still, the ordeal that I experienced with this employer affected to the point where I ended up in the ER suffering from emotional stress and anxiety attacks. Thank God I'm totally healed from that toxic couple. Whether the relationships are that of a lover, family, employer, in-laws, if it doesn't feel right, save yourself from the agony and run for the hills.

It is always good to go into a relationship one hundred percent, but always keep in mind "what ifs" whenever you are in a relationship. **If you feel like you are walking on eggshells, get out. If you feel you can't be yourself, get out. If you feel miserable, get out. If your partner can't be your best friend and confidant, get out. If there is no trust and horrible communication, get out.**

Everyone deserves peace, love, happiness, but the perfect mate is hard to find!

CHAPTER ONE

Getting Acquainted

I WAS BORN IN the Caribbean and came to this country twenty-eight years ago hoping for the American Dream. Upon coming to the United States, I moved to Brooklyn, where I lived as any New Yorker, dealing with the hustle and bustle of the city life. For twenty years, I woke up early in the morning and rushed to catch the train and then a bus. I would never miss those days, but I will always remember my humble beginnings and those crabs in a bucket experiences will forever keep me grounded.

Eight years ago, I moved to the suburbs, and I really loved the differences from the city. The scent of fresh air was invigorating. There was no concrete jungle feel. Absent was the noise from ambulances and gun shots. No longer did I have to wake up early in the morning to take a train with six hundred of my closest friends jammed into a train car. But the best thing of all was the lack of noisy neighbors. All that surrounded me was peace and tranquility.

For many years, I have worked as a nanny for mediocre folks to the rich and famous because I have a real passion for child care. It is my personal preference to care for children rather than deal with adults. When a child says, "I love you" to you, they mean it. Love is a misused word by adults. The love for family that is genuine and unconditional in most cases. However, the love from your employer, now, is conditional and can never be tied together like a ribbon.

Some years ago, I had an interview for a job in the city. I met a young couple, the Goldsteins. The husband, Connor, was tall, with dark hair, blue eyes, very handsome, and with a voice like George Clooney. The wife, Sharon, was also tall, with long blonde hair, blue eyes, very beautiful, and looked like a supermodel. Cindy was chubby, blue eyes, and very beautiful. She was also an extremely happy baby girl. The interview process went well, and I was hired to start work the following day. Everything went well, as everything always goes well in the beginning of any relationship. And so, after working a few weeks, I was asked by the couple if I was willing to move with them to the suburbs. I didn't mind because they seemed to be decent and genuine people who had a beautiful baby.

After speaking with my family, I took the offer and decided to move to New Jersey from Manhattan. And just like that, we all became a little family. When I mean *we*, I'm speaking of Sharon, Connor, Cindy, Charlie the dog, and myself.

I lived in their home six days a week. I went home to Brooklyn either on Saturday nights or early on Sunday mornings and returned back to work on Monday. Sharon didn't have much friends, and neither did I, so while Connor was working downstairs at night, Sharon would come to my room and we'd talk about the day to day events. As I got to know her, I told her more about myself, and as we got more acquainted, we hit it off rather well that a friendship began to bloom.

And that was when Sharon began to open up more about herself. She told me how Connor and her met, about his family, her childhood, her battle with depression, and of her situation of trying to commit suicide. Sharon would tell me of her parents, of how her mother always wanted things her way, and that her expectations were very high and failing was not an option in her parent's home.

We grew on each other and became comfortable talking with each other so much so that she began to offer me a glass of wine. That first time, I only took two sips and left the rest in the glass. I was at work, and it is important to me to always act in a professional manner at all times, especially in the presence of my employer. Sharon, on the other hand, would continue to pour glass after glass of wine until the bottle was empty. Each time she offered me a glass, I'd tell Sharon that I didn't like to drink, especially while on the job. I didn't like how it made my head feel, so I preferred not to drink. It is not something I'm comfortable doing around my employer.

One day, Sharon and I were sitting in the kitchen talking as we usually do and she said, "I don't know how long this marriage will last. Maybe a year or two." She made it clear to me what her intentions were. In the meanwhile, she'd stash away money so she can buy a house and live well. Sharon told me that Connor wanted more children, but she was not going to get pregnant for him again. She told him that due to his major birth defects, she didn't want to take any more chances and preferred to adopt. And with that said, she contacted an adoption agency and set up an interview.

A woman from the adoption agency came to the house and asked a series of questions about parentage to the prospective parents and the other person who was going to be in the adopted child's life. That was when Sharon called me into the interview process and introduced me to the lady. During the interview, Sharon said, "I have no intentions of being a 24/7 mother, so my nanny will be taking most of the active role in the child's life." Sharon later explained to the interviewer that she wanted to go back to being a career woman and didn't want that kind of commitment. So during the interview, the woman had me fill out an adoption form and did a background check on me. Now I'm thinking to myself, *I'm not financially stable to adopt a kid! Nor did I want that type of commitment for the next twenty-five years.* That's when I realized Sharon had flunked the interview on purpose . . . How clever! Just one of her tricks to throw Connor off to make him think she was all about having a well-settled family.

A couple of days went by, and the normal day to day activities in the house continued. Then one night during one of our nightly talks Sharon said, "I'm going to have Connor put all the properties in my name."

I replied, "Why would you do that? He is a businessman. He can handle it himself."

In which, Sharon said, "Carol, Connor gambles way too much. And besides, I need to secure me and Cindy's future, and I am not going to take any chances!"

From that point on, I noticed she wanted to have full control. Sharon was not joking when she said she was going to stash money away. Connor had business in Las Vegas, and he would have a private jet fly him back and forth with large amounts of money. Sharon, on the other hand, found out he was hiding money in the safe, so one night, while Connor was out, Sharon decided she was going to guess the combination number of his safe for the tenth time, and what do you know, bull's eye! She opened it. I stayed at the top of the stairs just shaking my head, and then I walked to the kitchen in disbelief. No sooner, I heard a tumble and a splat! "Oh my god! Sharon, are you all right?" I saw Sharon sprawled out at the bottom of the stairs with stacks of one hundred dollar bills all over the stairs and floor. Sharon answered, "I just broke my ass on those friggin' stairs." I couldn't help myself to hold back the laughter. She quickly gathered up the money and went upstairs. The next day, Sharon left the house early to go to the bank.

Connor's mother, Roberta, told Connor that Sharon was a shopaholic and wasting money. To my surprise, he told Roberta to mind her own business and stay out of his affairs. I said to myself, what an asshole. But by the end of the day, I'm just the nanny.

Since moving into the new house, Sharon had been having countless slip and fall accidents on the stairs. One of which, she had to have surgery in order to correct the problem. The house where we moved into was very huge, a whooping seven bedroom house with nine bathrooms, a pool, Jacuzzi, gym, theater, basketball court, and sauna. It was so large that you would think the house would be on that show where celebrities show off their houses. Sharon kept on slipping and falling so many times that her ankle would constantly be iced or taped up. Then she started complaining about her back. She would often come downstairs walking like a feeble old lady, as if she were one hundred years old and suffering from osteoporosis. But as soon as Connor left for work, she was fine. Strange and yet what an amazing recovery I would think or an academy award performance!

Anyway, she knew that I was onto her scheme, but I kept quiet. Yet again, it was not my business, and besides, I was only the nanny. Sharon continued her act from time to time. She would claim every week she had a doctor's appointment, ranging from your normal primary care physician, to chiropractor, to cosmetic doctor, to her shrink, and even a psychic, and on top of that, two physical trainers would come to the house. All these events would happen every single week. Her excuse for all of this was, "It'll help me get better if I keep active."

A couple of months past, and she claimed she started feeling much better, so she started swimming, biking, and running. Now, I'm all for someone getting in shape and looking good, but when you're in constant back pain and your ankle is taped up constantly, should you really be working out like an Olympian or doing triathlons? I don't think so.

A few months passed, when one day, she went shopping in the city and bought some very sexy yet beautiful clothes. She tried on several pieces for me to see. She was very particular about her clothes, which one should be, and I must say she dressed really nice. After seeing a particular outfit she wore, I said to her, "You look really smoking hot." Her response was, "Do I?" and I said, "You sure do. You look great!" Then she told me something, which I was shocked that a married person would say. "Carol, I'm going to the city to see my ex whom I haven't seen in a long time." Now, I don't know what her intentions were, but any woman in her right mind knows that if you're dressing sexy to see a man you haven't seen in a long time, then something is fishy with that picture. She then grabbed my hand and held my pinky finger as if we were little girls and said to me, "Swear to secrecy. Carol, you must never tell anyone. I mean no one." I replied, "It is not my business." And so she went on her secret hot date, returning the following afternoon.

I started to notice Sharon had a little bit of a drinking issue. She would crack open a bottle of wine and would drink the entire bottle as if it was water. She would drink a little more heavily when Connor was working. She would become extremely boisterous and slurred her speech, typical behavior of someone who was drunk. She'd talk negatively about his parents, especially his mother, but when his mom came to visit, she would run, hug her, and say, "I'm so happy to see you. I love you." Kisses and multiple hugs would be added after that statement. No sooner after, she would walk up the stairs, and you could hear her say, "That fucking Roberta. I can't stand her ass. I hope that bitch makes her visit short." The first time I heard her say that, I was absolutely stunned. I never said a word because at the end of the day, I'm only the nanny, the help, so I minded by business and kept focused on taking care of little Cindy. Sharon would spend little time with Cindy, and because of this, Cindy was very attached to me. I would give Cindy breakfast, lunch, and dinner, give her baths, and then put her to bed. Sharon would then walk into Cindy's room and give her a kiss on the cheek and then say goodnight. When Connor was home, he would always be there at night and teach Cindy her prayers. Connor had strong faith in God, and I respected that in him.

From time to time, Sharon will always volunteer information, a habit I realized she couldn't resist. Back in Brooklyn, the term for that is diarrhea mouth. Anyway, during one of our nightly talks, Sharon said, "Hey, Carol, he's coming to see me." I replied, "Who?" with a puzzled look on my face. "My friend from out of town, silly. I have to pack my overnight bag of sexy shit," she said.

I watched her packing her sexy lingerie as she happily talked as if she were doing nothing wrong. This "friend from out of town" came into town a lot throughout the entire marriage right under Connor's nose. She would tell Connor that she was going out for a girl's night out in the city but was in fact up to no good! After months of this behavior, she told Connor she wanted a divorce. She was not happy, and she couldn't take it anymore. After telling him about the divorce, Sharon partied every night coming home late all the time and neglecting her motherly role because she was tired from all her partying. And who was the one that suffered from all this? Cindy!

CHAPTER TWO

Secrets and Treachery

ONE MORNING, WHILE walking past the master bedroom I overheard Sharon yelling at the top of her lungs, "I want full custody of Cindy!" Connor's rebuttal to her demands was, "No, Sharon! Cindy is my child too, and I believe custody should be 50-50 split right down the middle. Both parents should be in her life, and your idiotic demands are freaking ridiculous."

For the rest of the day, I pretended to be impervious of what was going on. I started to fear for my job. In my line of work, when couples split, it meant fewer hours for the nanny in most cases. But my most important worry was for Cindy. No child should have to see their parents battling each other during a divorce.

Later that night, Sharon and I had our nightly talk. She told me she lived in Miami for a number of years and that was where she fell in love with her ex; however, he was cheating on her. She then made a confession, "After I found out he cheated on me, I stalked him."

My reply to that was, "What! Are you crazy? You know people get in trouble for stalking."

"Hey, Carol, he was black, and you know, I couldn't resist," she said.

"Okay, what couldn't you resist, Sharon?"

"Carol, don't play stupid. You're black, so you should know. Besides, the guy was laying down serious pipe. The sex was epic with him. I mean hours."

I couldn't help but chuckle a bit. It was very funny to hear your boss talk about her past sex life. She told me how heartbroken she was after they broke up, and it had brought on a little depression. I pitied her because when someone loves another person, no one should be cheated on. I've experienced being cheated on, and it is no laughing matter.

Later in the conversation, she told me how she and Connor reconnected. Apparently, they both had a mutual friend, and she heard from this friend that Connor was now rich and doing fine. Sharon then said something extremely twisted, "When I heard that he was rich, I said to myself, 'Fuck it! Never mind his handicap. He is a rich son of a gun.'" I suddenly became sick to my stomach at hearing this because her intentions were as clear as purified water. She continued with her story, telling me they dated a while, and then not long after, they got married. Shortly after, she got pregnant with Cindy, which according to her was a huge risk.

"Why was it a huge risk? Connor is a good looking guy—tall and handsome. And you're a beautiful woman. I would think the baby would come out like a supermodel."

"Carol, because of Connor's, how should I say this, fucked up genes, it was a risk. He has major birth defects. Who wants to deal with that fucking shit! Besides, his whole damn family has fucked up genes. His father, his mother, and oh, yes, his sisters too have that retarded gene."

I was starting to be a little inquisitive about the matter, but in the back of my mind, I always knew his family to be nice, warm people with limitless love whenever they came around, especially his mother. Sharon continued her rant, "His sisters, those bitches, have some nerve if they think their family has some rich relative in Connor. Because I have Cindy, he won't need those three assholes. Cindy and I are his family now." Suddenly she got up. "Goodnight, Carol," she said, then stumbled down the hallway and into one of the many bedrooms, leaving an empty bottle of wine behind in my room.

One day, Sharon was hanging out in the kitchen making a sandwich when the doorbell rang. Since I was in the foyer, I looked through the peephole and saw a gentleman I've never seen before. I opened the door and asked who he was looking for. He said he was looking for someone named Sharon. I yelled, "Sharon, someone is at the door for you." The stranger turned out to be the furniture delivery man, who was tall, dark haired, olive skinned, and from the white t-shirt he wore, you could tell he worked out. In his simple attire of faded jeans, t-shirt, and boots, he was, nonetheless, a handsome guy.

As he was bringing the furniture through the front door, it was quite noticeable that Sharon was checking him out. I said not a word and pretended to mind my business. Then after the furniture was brought in, she engaged him in a conversation, which I played a fly on the wall.

Looking at his name tag she said, "Jason."

"Yes, ma'am," he replied.

"Don't call me ma'am. Call me Sharon."

"Okay Sharon. How can I help you?"

"I must say you are an attractive drink of water, Jason."

"Oh, thank you."

"Mind if I call you Jay?"

"Not at all, Sharon."

"I can tell that you workout, Jay. You have a nice body. You're good looking, and you're sexy."

"Well, thank you. I'm flattered."

She then asked him if he does "private jobs," and she'd like to have him work for her. I started to think this lady is nuttier than squirrel shit. Who in the hell flirts in their husband's house, especially when their husband is several rooms down the hall working in his office. This made me look at her in disgust.

One weekend, Connor had gone into the city for a guy's weekend out. So it was Sharon, Cindy, and I for a girl's weekend. I decided to stay in New Jersey for the weekend. After I put Cindy to bed, Sharon grabbed a bottle of wine and began her nightly routine. I was eating ice cream as she drank, and after two glasses, the conversation went from movies on *Lifetime* and *WE* to her personal life.

"Hey, Carol, did you ever notice Connor's feet?"

"No, I never noticed his feet for a matter of fact."

"Carol, Carol, oh my god, when I look at his feet, I feel like I have to vomit."

I left the matter alone and pretended I never heard a word she said. There was soon a silence in the room for a short while as she was busy texting God knows who on her phone, until she startled me by saying, "I know you're worried about your job. Connor will give me the divorce but have no fear. I'll have enough money to keep you around until Cindy goes to college."

I listened to her and a little relief came over me. The idea of moving to New Jersey from Brooklyn and leaving my family and all that I knew behind to come here with this family only to lose my job because of this crazy bitch was unnerving. It would have been a waste of my time and for those who know me well know that my time is the most precious thing to me. I digested what she said mentally and replied, "But, Sharon, Cindy is small, and she loves her daddy."

Her reply was, "Yes, I know. He is a great father and a good provider, and he adores her. I will never, ever deprive Connor from seeing Cindy because he is a good man, and I know I'll never be able to find another man to love me like Connor does."

"So, Sharon, why are you divorcing him? If he is a good man."

"Carol, Connor puts the capital B in boring. I quicker get an orgasm watching paint dry than sleeping with Connor, and besides, I must make my move now when Cindy is young so it would be less painful for her."

That following week Connor's parents came to visit. It was the ending of May, and they had come to visit because Cindy had a ballet recital. One afternoon, while everyone was out, Sharon and I sat at the kitchen table, and she went on and on about her new house when I interjected by saying, "I can't believe you are actually leaving your husband. What would his family, his parents, think? His parents love you and look at you as a daughter, and Connor loves you a great deal. You are going to ruin them emotionally! You should reconsider divorcing him and save your marriage."

At that moment, Connor walked into the kitchen and busied himself with getting food from the pantry and walking back and forth through the kitchen to notice the look of disgust on Sharon's face. As we sat there, Sharon said, "Look at him. He's so disgusting and retarded and annoying. I can't believe I married him." A shocking statement.

As I lay in bed one night, I was reminiscing about another one of our episodes. Last fall, on one of my days off, Sharon invited me to go shopping to buy new clothes for Cindy. That afternoon, Sharon and I dropped Cindy at her mother's home, and during our drive to the mall Sharon strike up a conversation. "One night, I got really drunk—a little fucked up drunk, and passed out. I woke a little late the following day."

"Okay, where are you going with this?" I said.

"Well, Carol, you remember Sophia my sister from Thanksgiving dinner?"

"Yes, I do."

"Okay, well, Sophia asked me where was Cindy? I said to her she was sleeping. You know, Carol, she had some nerve to say I am not a responsible mother!"

Sharon was upset with Sophia for months on end, and both were not on speaking terms. I've heard through the grapevine that Sophia told Sharon that she needed to take it easy on the drinking, for fear that Sharon may be becoming an alcoholic. I also remember many times Sharon reached out to Sophia during the holidays and family gatherings, and Sophia elected not to come. I guess to the fact that she didn't respect her sister. Their mother, Jill, would go to Sophia's home, pick her kids up, and bring them to the house for birthday parties and other family gatherings. To my knowledge during my conversations with Sharon, Sophia didn't want to be her sister nor her friend, and the only thing, according to Sophia, that connected her to Sharon was the fact that they are blood-related. I guess in this case, water is thicker than the blood they shared. As I lay in bed ready to literally pass out from the heavy weight on my mind, I couldn't help but think of all the negative shit that was surrounding me. Here I was, living with a successful family, and yet they were still acting childish.

That following morning, during breakfast, Sharon announced, "Since Connor and I are going to be going separate ways, here is the plan. When I have Cindy, you'll be with me, and when Connor has her, you'll be with him. The only downside is you'll have to go back and forth since I will be moving out."

"No problem. So it's safe to say, my hours are intact?"

"Yup, it is Carol. You have nothing to worry about. I am not going to lose you. Cindy loves you dearly, and besides, I rather go on a hunger strike than have you leave us. I even told my lawyer this on Friday!" She assured me over and over that my job was safe and kept on telling me to relax. But the fact that she had given me a hint that she had already seen a lawyer gave me a calm before the storm sort of feeling.

CHAPTER THREE

Motherhood

I STARTED FEELING as if my job was becoming more of a burden than that of a hobby. Sharon would have me run errands, take care of Cindy, cook, and do a lot of miscellaneous stuff around the house. As for cooking, I realized they fell in love with my cooking, so I became the unofficial chief of the house, which I didn't mind one bit. Sharon, on the other hand, did not care if Connor ate, drank, or slept, only if he continued to bring in money. Her main concerns were that of Cindy and her dog, Charlie. She would often call Conner "Money Bags," a nickname I secretly detested due to the fact that she looked at Connor as a material object, and he looked at her as his wife.

I recalled a few weeks ago, I made fish for dinner, and Sharon enjoyed it, saying to me, "Carol, this fish was the bomb, and if that idiot comes home, hide the fish. Don't give him any! Let him eat the leftover fried chicken from last night in the fridge."

"Sharon, there is enough fish for him. When he comes home, I am going to make him a plate."

The expression she gave me was one of the utmost displeasure as if I committed a sin in the eyes of God. Around nine o'clock that night, I heard the custom knock on my bedroom door.

"Come on in, Sharon."

She sat on my ottoman with her favorite drinking partner, a bottle of wine. She was never greedy with her wine, always offering me, but I always refused. That night, we talked about her several attempts at suicide. She also expressed that she had been diagnosed with ADHD and Bipolar disorder. My knowledge of ADHD was extremely limited, yet I didn't judge her because it was not in my nature to judge someone about their illness or mental health. She expressed that she was a very depressed woman and that her doctor had her on medicine for her depression, which I pitied her. As the saying goes, money doesn't bring happiness. Here you have someone who practically has everything—money, cars, a beautiful family, a great big home—and still she was missing something.

I began to notice Sharon's extreme moodiness. I guess that's one of the side effects of being bipolar. She would often have crazy mood swings, and I would often ignore it due to the fact that I didn't want to put any more stress on myself than what I was being paid for. The mood swings got so bad it often affected her parenting toward Cindy, making Sharon's patience very limited and causing her to yell at Cindy for petty things or even giving her timeouts for the most absurd things. I am all for disciplining a child, but I believe in respecting your child and speaking to your child with respect versus talking down and being mean. There were many times when Sharon and Cindy would get into it, and Cindy would run into the bathroom and lock the door yelling, "Stop it! Stop it! Mom, I don't want to talk to you."

Sharon was rarely home, and I had to pick up the load, which made me feel more like Cindy's mother. Sharon would often tell me, "Carol, I have to go see this lawyer and that lawyer. I am going to fight for Cindy." I guess now that the custody battle was in full swing, let the games begin! During that time period, Sharon would constantly call me and text me. I started getting annoyed, especially one time when she texted me while I was driving. Her constant annoyance was something new and which she never did in the past. Even Cindy started noticing. One day, while driving her back from school, the phone started to ring, and Cindy yelled from the back seat, "Carol, Carol, if that's my mommy, don't answer."

"Cindy, sweetie, I need to pick up."

"No, Carol. All mommy does is yell and yell, and she's going to be mad."

Sharon would constantly yell at Cindy. At times, she would pull Cindy into a vacant bedroom and yell at her. Then Cindy would come crying to me. One evening, the yelling got so bad that Cindy came running into my arms saying, "All I wanted to do was ask mommy a question, but she is always busy." Many times, Sharon would pressure Cindy into doing activities she wasn't very keen on doing.

I remembered one occasion, Cindy woke up very early, and by ten o'clock in the morning, she wanted to take a nap. Sharon insisted Cindy go outside and play. I got involved and said, "Sharon, allow her to nap. When she wakes up, let her play and tire herself. This way she can be on her normal sleep schedule, and she'd get a good night's rest."

"Carol, don't tell me what to do."

Five minutes later, Sharon starts yelling at Cindy to go outside and play. Cindy then has a tantrum and Sharon started yelling, "Quit crying. You are being a brat and being rude. Go to your room this instant!" And then I saw the strangest thing. After Sharon's outburst, she grabbed Cindy then spanked her a couple of times. As soon as her mother's grip loosened, Cindy ran away to her room, I assumed. Twenty minutes later, I went to check up on Cindy, and she was fast asleep in her bed. Poor kid, all she wanted to do was sleep.

I told Sharon, "You need to listen to your child."

"Well, Carol, I am trying to be the best mother I can be. I'm trying to discipline her, but it seems like I keep fucking up. Please help me! What am I doing wrong?"

As I was about to comment on her question, she interjects with, "I am afraid for you to talk to the lawyers."

"Why would you be afraid? Besides, why would they want to talk to me? And if they do, I'll have to speak the truth."

"Oh, Carol. Oh, Carol," Sharon started crying, saying my name over and over again. "Oh, Carol. Oh, Carol . . . What can I do to make things right? If it's the money, I can give two shits."

"Well, for starters, Sharon, Cindy is in a stable environment. By you uprooting her from that stability, that is unstable. Her mind is still developing and seeing her mom and dad apart will not be easy on her. Children tend to not understand these things because their minds are so fragile, and you are taking her to a new home."

"Well, Carol, I always liked new shit as a kid. I understand the part about not being able to be with her dad, but I don't love Connor! What the fuck you expect me to do? Be with someone I can't stand? Someone who annoys the living shit out of me?"

I said nothing. I kept my mouth shut. *Mum's the word*, I thought in the back of my head.

She started off again, "What can I do to be a better mom, Carol!"

I thought to myself, *a just and honest question*. Then I replied, "Sharon, when a woman gives birth to a child, an instruction manual does not pop out too. Parenting is a hard job! And it's not what you say, but it's how you say it! Communication is vital between child and parent. And even if Cindy doesn't want to do something, you, as the parent, Sharon, must gradually introduce it to her and guide her in a positive direction without being demanding on her because that'll only make Cindy frustrated and rebellious, and that could hinder the relationship between mother and daughter."

"Thanks for the advice, Carol. You know, that asshole told his lawyers that I'm not a mother to Cindy. You believe that son of a bitch. Anyway, fuck him. I'm going for a bike ride."

"Sharon, you shouldn't go for a bike ride. I advise you it's not a good idea because you're a little upset. You should go upstairs and lay down. A nap is always a good way to recharge your batteries." To my surprise, she took my advice.

Every day, she would remind me about her moving out to the point of it started to become annoying. It was as if she was a broken record. On one occasion during our nightly talks, she turned to me and said, "When I asked Connor for a divorce, I thought honestly he would've packed all his shit and move out of the house. You know, Carol, he's not budging one bit. Why wouldn't he fucking leave?" She looked at me expecting an answer, so I gave her one that she wasn't expecting.

"Well, Sharon, it's both yours and Connor's house. Why don't you guys sleep in different rooms? The house is big enough for both of you." With that statement, I got a look of disgust, as if she wanted to say, "shut the fuck up," but she didn't want to say it since I was her only friend. Besides, she did not want to get her only friend upset with her, especially when I knew all her dirt.

The environment I've come to love was quickly being destroyed as if a sinkhole was beneath the soil of our relationship. Every day it was becoming more like the War of Roses and each time Roberta, Connor's mother, would visit, Sharon would look at me with a look of distaste and whispers, "That motherfucking Roberta. I can't stand her ass."

"Why, Sharon? Roberta is a sweetheart."

"Carol, she talks and talks and talks, and she won't shut up. I don't mind her visits. But she overstays her fucking welcome."

Roberta lives out of state and rarely visits, so why would Sharon harbor such feelings for a person who was very kind and sweet to her and treated her like a daughter? I started noticing something about Sharon. She was always talking badly about Connor's family—from his parents to his sisters. I remember her saying to me that Connor's sister Joslyn needed to go on a diet and lose weight because she had a fat ass. In some cultures, men love women with big butts and a little extra meat on their bones, and at the end of the day, it was about the person and not how they appeared on the outside.

One day after lunch, Sharon and I decided to take Cindy to the park. We had an early lunch. The day was still young, and it was beautiful out. The sky was a vivid blue, and the birds were out and yet all I could think of was, *I hope this woman doesn't ruin a beautiful day.* When we got to the park, Cindy ran to the sandbox while Sharon and I sat on the bench watching the other children there with their guardians playing. I was admiring the magnificence of the day when, out of nowhere, Sharon started with, "Carol, when am done divorcing Moneybags, I'll be getting a lump sum of money from him, and I'm going to buy a house."

"Okay."

"That's all you have to say, Carol, is okay! Anyway, I want you to move in with me. The house I am buying will be so huge. I want you to have your own floor."

"Wow, Sharon, that's awesome." I pretended as if I was there in the conversation, but mentally, I wasn't. I was sick and tired of her excessive scheming and plotting.

She turned to me and said, "So are you going to move in with me? Because I want you and I to raise Cindy like a lesbian couple. Yup, you and me, Carol, raising Cindy like a lesbian family, and there is nothing wrong with Cindy having two mothers."

I was a bit shocked, but I replied, "Okay," hoping it would shut her up. I also started realizing this lady was crazy! Crazy enough to pull this off. She had more courage than most men, a crazy yet twisted, ballsy kind of courage, nonetheless.

During our drive back to the house, Cindy was fast asleep in her car seat, and there was dead silence except for the subtle noises of traffic, when Sharon said, "Carol, can I trust you?"

"Sharon, you trust me with taking care of your child, so what do you think?"

"Okay, Carol. I filed for divorce."

I was stunned, yet not surprised. Nothing honestly surprised me because of the things Sharon said, and I knew one day her mouth would get her in trouble, yet my simple, honest answer was, "How do you feel?"

"Awesome," she replied without a second thought.

I started to feel at times as if I were a character in a movie, and that there was always a plot, always an agenda with Sharon, always a scheme. Now Connor's other sister Jessica started becoming close to me. Anytime she visited, she would take me for lunch, and we'd talk first about life in general then she'd begin to try and get information on Sharon's schemes, but I kept my mouth shut on what I might have known. She was very frank with me about her brother's condition as if she was trying to get me to sympathize. Jessica, who was always suspicious of Sharon, told me to keep an eye on her because she believed that Sharon was up to no good from day one. Even if her brother didn't see it due to his blindness by love and lust for Sharon, Jessica seemed to be distrustful of her. One night, during Sharon's yapping of her schemes and plots, I recalled what Jessica had told me of Connor's health condition, and I, knowing of what Sharon was doing, knew he would be devastated, and the stress would probably kill him. I was at a mental crossroads in my life. Should I bite the hand that feeds me and not tell Connor about Sharon's scheming? Or should I stand up for what was right? I was never one to sell my soul for riches and knowing of what Sharon was planning made me a co-conspirator. I had to clear my name before what was in the dark came into the light. I decided to act, and in doing so, it meant I had to tell Jessica.

I decided to make that phone call to Jessica when no one was home. Sharon had gone on a dinner date with friends, and Connor had gone to his office in New York. It was only Cindy and I in the house, and Cindy was fast asleep in her bed, so it was the perfect opportunity to call Jessica.

Now, before calling Jessica, I had a good angel versus bad angel moment. You know that moment when you're indecisive over a moral dilemma? Well, I was having that moment while staring at the phone. Morally, you know what you're doing is right. But at the same time, I felt like this act of goodwill would come back and kick me in the ass. I shoved the bad angel aside and made the phone call to Jessica. I just could not let Sharon's plan create any negative impact on Connor's health, nor could I allow Cindy to lose her father. Besides, I could not personally live with myself if I stood at the sidelines and watch as Sharon destroy a good man.

I had to clear my name and all involvement of Sharon's schemes without getting involved with their legal battle. I quickly realized that she was wheeling me in to be on her side of lies, and this situation started to haunt me, knowing full well that if this reaches the court, I will have to commit perjury for Sharon.

"I'm sorry, but that bitch is on her own."

"I am too old to make jail"

During my conversation with Jessica, I made it known to her that I did not want to be in any part of Sharon's malicious plan. I explained to her of what Sharon's plans were from the beginning, of how she wedded Connor and bedded him, getting knocked up, and then going for the jugular which was Connor's finances. I explained to Jessica of how I was saddened by the entire ordeal and how I believed Sharon's deeds were wrong and heartless. I guess another reason why I opened my mouth and said something to Jessica was because Connor's family were great people and still are, and they didn't deserve that kind of gratitude from Sharon's premeditated plans.

My mother always told my siblings and I that being deceitful was far worse than witchcraft. And as I explained to Jessica all of what was going on, she was stunned. I felt as if during our phone conversation she suspected of Sharon's capabilities, yet she underestimated her. As Jessica and I ended our conversation, and she thanked me for giving her the inside scoop. I hope what I did wouldn't bite me in my ass.

CHAPTER FOUR

Carol's Realization

MY OUTLOOK ON Sharon was that of a woman who was cunning, wicked, seductive, and manipulative. Deep inside, I knew this about her all along, and yet I chose to ignore her behavioral traits because I liked to believe that people couldn't really be like this.

As weeks progressed, Sharon started using the term "we" quite often in her vocabulary. It was as if she decided to infuse French with English. I would often hear her say, "We are taking all the antique furniture. And we're taking all the silverware. And we're taking the Tiffany and Faberge dishes." Her constant excessive use of the word "we" made me tell her one afternoon, "I don't speak French." I guess the reason why she'd used the term "we" so much was because she thought I was her Pinky and she was the Brain. Well, I am nobody's Pinky!

My mother always told me, "One smart always outsmart two smarts." For this reason, I called Jessica. I had nothing to do with Sharon's plots even though I was mentioned in her plans in regards of moving in with her. But I was no co-conspirator!

At this point, all of her thoughts seemed to revolve around playing some sort of mental chess. What will her next move in her grand plot to screw over Connor be? I could only imagine what sinister schemes were going on in that bloody brain of hers, and I often wondered if Connor was smart enough to have drawn up a prenuptial agreement with this Looney Tune of a character soon to be his ex-wife.

As weeks progressed, I noticed Sharon's parenting style started to change. She started listening to Cindy a lot more and paying a little more attention to her needs. I guess she was getting her "Mommy act together" because there was a custody battle on the horizon.

One day, Cindy was being very moody. Everything you did or suggested made her very uncooperative to the point where she was being very mean and rude. And as I was attempting to give her a timeout, when I heard out of nowhere, "Cindy, honey, it's okay to be rebellious. And anytime you feel upset, grab a pillow and scream into it." Upon hearing this, my jaw dropped. Of course, I wasn't surprised to hear that it was Sharon who was saying such idiocy.

Cindy's innocent response to this was, "Okay, Mommy."

Several hours later, Sharon and I were sitting in her office sipping tea as if we were Aristocrats. By the way, I never understood why Sharon had an office in the first place. She never worked since she got involved with Connor from what she told me and, of course, from my observations.

She asked me, "Carol, how is my parenting lately? I am listening."

I couldn't help notice the part when she was telling Cindy about being rebellious and had to address it. "Well, you did take my advice about listening, but you still did not get it quite right honestly."

"What do you mean by honestly, Carol?"

"Okay, Sharon, you want my honest opinion? Here it is. It is never okay for a parent to tell a child it is okay to be rebellious. It is wrong! You don't want a rebellious child on your hands. A rebellious child can be a major headache for a parent. And as Cindy becomes older, by you telling her it's okay to be rebellious at her tender age, will only cost you a major headache in the future especially when she gets into her teens, so watch what you say and how you say it because a child never forgets."

With that, she sat back behind her Oakwood desk and looked as though deep in thought. I continued to sip on my tea, minding my business, deep in thought myself, thinking of all the mothers I have worked with in my profession. And by far, Sharon was the worst communicator of the bunch. I've always believed in the old saying, "It takes a village to raise a child," and although we were far from the village mentality, Sharon understood that she needed my help in regards to raising Cindy, which I was fully capable of doing.

A couple of weeks had passed since our little conversation. She took my advice and made more of an effort to parent Cindy; however, it seemed as if she heard me but had not listened. I begged her to change her approach and communication tactics with Cindy, but yet again my words fell on deaf ears.

It was Labor Day weekend, and I had the next two days off. I woke up on Sunday and decided to take advantage of the picture-perfect day and head down to Brooklyn early to spend time with my family. I said my goodbyes to Sharon and Cindy, making sure all was well.

On my drive back up to New Jersey on Monday evening, I was reminiscing on all the festivities, the color of the costumes I saw at the West Indian Day Parade, the flavors and spices of the Caribbean dishes, and all the fun I had with my family. I had really enjoyed my time off and felt refreshed and ready to go back to work.

As I pulled into the driveway of the gigantic house in New Jersey, I could see the brand new BMW Coupe owned by Sharon's mother, Jill, parked outside the house. While walking into the house, I thought to myself that the environment would be different with Jill here.

That was when I saw Cindy lying on the sofa. She looked so pale and out of it. I walked into the kitchen and said to Sharon, "Goodnight, Sharon and Jill. Hope all is well with you ladies. Sharon, what is wrong with Cindy? She is very silent and looks pale and not her usual self."

"Oh, hey, Carol. Cindy is not feeling well. She didn't eat or drink all day."

With that comment, I thought to myself, *this woman is either impervious to her child's behavior or she is dumber than a doornail. Let's go with choice two.* I went back into the living room to check on Cindy. I brushed the back of my hand under her chin and felt her forehead and felt she had a temperature. I turned around, and there was Sharon looking at me. I asked her if Cindy ate or drank the day before, which she told me Cindy hadn't eaten nor did she drink anything since the Sunday I left. I expressed to Sharon that it was urgent that we take her to the hospital because she looked dehydrated. Sharon's rebuttal to this, "Okay! But Carol, I called the doctor and left a message on his voicemail. We're still waiting to hear from him."

I decided to take matters into my own hands and jumped in the car and drove straight to the pharmacy. I bought two bottles of Pedialyte and speed back to the house. I attempted to feed Cindy, but after an hour and a half, when she still did not eat anything, I begged Sharon to take her to the hospital. At that moment, Jill walked into the room and suggested to Sharon to take my advice. Jill was the voice of reason in this scenario because Sharon could be very stubborn at times.

We left immediately to the hospital where we found out that Cindy came down with a case of pneumonia. She was hospitalized for three days. On that Thursday, Cindy was discharged from the hospital, and instead of a simple thank you, which I didn't expect because I was doing my job, all I got was, "It's your fault! It's your freaking fault Cindy got sick! You shouldn't have left for Brooklyn!"

"So, Sharon, you're telling me I shouldn't have days off? I shouldn't spend time with my family? Are you kidding me! You are her mother! I watch Cindy six days a week! She is your child, and you need to spend time with her!"

"But, Carol, I called you! You had a right to come back!"

"Sharon, I never got your call, and if I did, I would've returned your call immediately!" And with that, I silenced her immediately because she knew I would have answered her call. Each time she called me, I picked up like some kind of lackey. At this point, my realization came very clear. I didn't know if she thought I was an indentured servant or just a dunce waiting for her beck and call. But I am no one's push over.

After our little debacle, I started realizing it was mostly Connor or I putting Cindy to bed because every night Sharon would be downstairs on the phone yapping away or making secret investments with some of Connor's money she stashed away while he was preparing Cindy for bed. And when she wasn't in the house at nights, Sharon would either be hanging out with friends or seeing her *special friend* from out of town. I personally believed that Sharon wasn't prepared to be a wife nor a mother.

So one day, I decided to sit down and talk with her about how I felt in regards to her spending more time with Cindy. I explained to her that my work hours were killing me mentally and draining me physically because I felt as if I was doing everything for Cindy, and Sharon wasn't contributing at all. Now the crazy part of the conversation with Sharon happened when I explained to her that I needed to have a life other than being there for Cindy 24/7.

I said to her, "Sharon, I need to have a life. That doesn't mean when you say jump, I should say how high."

Sharon gave me a peculiar look. She cocked her eyes, paused, and then said, "I expect you to jump to the moon."

With that comment, I excused myself from the room respectively and went for a drive. My job was becoming demanding, pressured, and frustrating. Dealing with someone whom had ADHD and Bipolar disorder and who wasn't on medication most of the time was a cocktail for a great migraine. Sharon's bizarre behavior only continued to get worse. I knew her doctor insisted she take her medication, but my hypothesis on the matter was either she wasn't taking the medicine or the bitch was just too damn crazy for the medicine to help.

I recalled one afternoon while watching TV in the living room when Sharon came in and yelled, "Damn, Carol! You're always watching Oprah! I am fed up of Oprah! Oprah this and Oprah that!"

"Have you ever met Oprah, Sharon?" I said calmly.

Her reply was, "No!"

In my head, I'm thinking, t*hen why would you be so negative toward a person you haven't met.* I explained to Sharon there was no need to be negative toward Oprah Winfrey because she is a respected and positive person, who has opened doors for many people. She continued to rant about the show, and I simply picked up the remote control and aimed it at her while she wasn't looking and pressed the mute button. What I honestly wanted to say was, "Shut the hell up!" but I was working and living in her home, and I had to conduct myself in a professional manner.

Sharon's mood swings were a mental beat down to anyone around her. She would be the sweetest person at times, and I missed that side of her a lot. We'd joke around, go shopping, and have great conversations. But then at the snap of your fingers, her demeanor would change. Her eyes would open up extremely wide, and communication would become an impossible task. And on many occasions, when family members would visit, they would secretly praise me for the changes they seen in Sharon. If only they knew!

My job continued with some of the mental abuse that came with it. It started off very minor, but only time could tell if the mental abuse would stop or proceed. One incident made me walk off the job. Sharon's family came to the house to spend the weekend. On Saturday morning, Sharon gave Cindy a bagel and cream cheese for breakfast. I had noticed that two mornings before, she had given Cindy the same breakfast, and due to the lack of fiber in Cindy's diet she was becoming constipated, so I took it upon myself to give Cindy a little prune juice to help relieve her so her bowel movements would become normal again. That night, while everyone was sleeping, Cindy had a very big bowel movement that seeped through her diaper and onto the bed sheets. Since Sunday I was off duty, I was not called upon to help clean up the mess, but later that day, I was called into Sharon's "office." We sat down and she started the conversation a little jittery as if something was bothering her, and boy was my ears in for a treat.

"Carol, did you give Cindy a laxative?"

"Yes and no. I gave her prune juice because she was constipated."

"You fucking bitch!" Sharon screamed at me.

My eyes opened wide as I stared at her in shock. I did not know how to respond to that. All I could say was, "What!"

She quickly replied, "You heard me, Carol! Carol, I had to clean up all that shitty mess all morning. YOU'RE SO LUCKY YOU GOT AWAY BECAUSE IT'S YOUR DAY OFF. NEXT TIME SOMETHING LIKE THIS HAPPENS, I AM HEADING STRAIGHT FOR YOUR ROOM AND HAVE YOU CLEAN IT! UNFUCKING BELIEVABLE!"

And with that comment, I stormed out of her office, went to my room, and packed my things. I told everyone I was leaving. Connor's face seemed puzzled as to what was going on when I left. But I guess Cruella de Vil didn't mention what took place. After a day or two, I got a phone call from Sharon. She apologized and I accepted her apology. She told me to come back to the house because Cindy missed me. How could I not come back? I really bonded with Cindy. She was a sweet and beautiful little girl.

A couple of weeks after Sharon a.k.a. Cruella de Vil disrespected me, I started looking for apartments in the surrounding area of their residence. I found a one bedroom townhouse then explained to the Goldsteins why I was moving out. I felt as if when I was at work I had no freedom. Besides, I could not have family visit nor could they sleep over even though I knew the Goldsteins wouldn't mind my family staying since they had enough spare bedrooms. However, I didn't want my children or other family members staying in the house with Sharon as a ticking time bomb. So I moved fifteen minutes away. Now every morning, I would be at work at eight and wake up Cindy, give her breakfast, and prepare her for school. When school was on break, I'd wake her up normal time and prepare her for the day activities such as play dates and horseback riding. Anyway, one morning, Sharon asked me to come into the study of their home. We sat down, and she held my hand. She said to me, "Carol, I appreciate all you do for us, but I will no longer be needing you for child care. However, I want you to be the manager for the house. Because I can't make a final decision in regards to child care, you'll be allowed in my home between the hours of 10:00 a.m. and 2:00 p.m."

I quickly pulled my hand away from that Judas of a woman and said, "I am a bit taken aback and shocked. If you knew you were going to terminate me, why the hell you told me to come back several weeks ago? What is the reason for my termination?"

"Well, Carol, here are the reasons. For telling me I had 'serious issues,' for your increasing history of not following orders and directives, and last but certainly not least, not being forthcoming with information about activities when specifically asked, especially recent occurrences." And with that, she looked at me and smiled.

CHAPTER FIVE

Mind Games

AT THIS POINT, I started spending less time with Cindy than I normally did. Yet when I was needed to care for her, I was always there. For instance, during the autumn, there was a Nor'easter which hit the East Coast. It was a pretty bad storm. There were a lot of downed trees and coastal flooding. Hundreds were affected by the severe weather, which caused blackouts due to downed trees. During the storm, I heard multiple bangs on my door. I suddenly had a fright run through my body. How could I not be afraid? I was alone during a storm an entire state away from my family. Nervously, I walked to the door. But being a good hearted person, I summed up the courage because I feared someone may be in danger. With my heart racing, I looked through the peephole. And who should I see standing there wet and helpless? Sharon! I opened the door to my house.

Sharon said, "Thank you, Carol. Thank you. I know you have power. I was listening to all the affected areas with an old battery radio I found in the garage. I knew your town had power so I called all the local hotels, but they are all booked up. I haven't had power for five days, and our generator blew out. And as you know, Connor is stuck in LA on a business trip. He can't get a flight into JFK due to the weather."

"No problem. Sure come in. Where is Cindy?"

"I'll go back to the car and get her and Charlie." She quickly ran back to her car and got Cindy and the dog as I held the front door open. That night, I treated Sharon as one of my family. I gave up the comforts of my bed to her and Cindy while I slept downstairs on the futon in my living room, which was very uncomfortable. As I laid down listening to the wind whistling, my mind drifted on Sharon—on how she fired me for being there for her daughter and caring for her. Sharon's relationship with me was far more than that of an employee/employer relationship. Sharon would always ask for my opinion in important decisions. We would do things together like we were the best of friends, and now, it was as if she was only someone who existed and not a friend.

The next day, Sharon left to visit friends in LA. She claimed it was work related, so I had Cindy for the days she left. A couple of days later, I received a call from Sharon telling me her flight was delayed, and she was not sure what time she'd arrive at the house. In the meanwhile, Connor came back from his trip and had asked me to go food shopping, so as usual Cindy and I went to the grocery store. While at the grocery store, I bought ice cream for Cindy, and we had fun spending time together.

Then Sharon called. "Where are you?"

"I'm at the grocery store."

"I'm in the car on my way home."

"How soon will you be home?" I asked her.

"In about an hour and fifteen minutes if traffic is good."

"Okay, see you soon."

Fifty minutes later, Sharon called again. "Carol, I'll be home in about half an hour."

"Okay, I'll see you home." I placed my phone back in my bag and was busy helping the cashier pack the groceries in the cart. I put the groceries in the trunk and put Cindy in her car seat. Before I could turn the ignition of the car, Sharon called again.

"Carol, where are you?"

"I'm getting ready to leave the grocery store."

"I miss my baby. I'm coming to meet you. Which grocery store are you at?"

"What's the point of you driving here when I'll be there in a few minutes?" With that I hung up the phone and drove to the house.

When I reached the property, Sharon came running toward the car while it was still in motion. She opened the car door and lifted Cindy out of the car seat. I popped the trunk and began taking the groceries out when Sharon asked, "Did you tell Connor that I was on my way home?"

"No, I did not."

"Huh. Well, did he tell you to go to the grocery after he found out I was on my way home?"

"No, Sharon. Oh! You didn't tell him you were on your way? I only found out you were on your way while I was at the grocery store."

"I don't care if you have to leave the groceries on the checkout counter just be where I want you to be."

Sharon was never the one to show so much concern about Cindy's whereabouts, but now she was becoming a pain in the ass. For all the years I worked for this family, I was never late, and when Cindy was with me, I was always within a phone calls reach.

One day, I took Cindy to the Aquarium for a fun afternoon out. While there, Connor called to speak to Cindy. She told him where we were, and he asked her if she wanted to visit daddy's new office. She got all excited saying, "Yes, yes. Carol, please take me to daddy's new office."

"Okay, let me talk to your daddy."

"Carol, please come by. It's only five minutes away."

We arrived at Connor's office, and the receptionist called Connor to announce our arrival. He came out to the front desk, lifted Cindy, kissed her, and walked her through his office to show her off to meet his colleagues. The entire visit lasted about three minutes, and then we left. When we got back to the house, Sharon was in her office on a conference call. She asked that I keep Cindy away while she was in the office, so I gave Cindy dinner and a bath. While reading her a bedtime story, Connor came home from work. He asked where Sharon was. I told him she was downstairs in her office (working on her scheming plans, if only he knew). Connor told me I could go home, and he'll take over with Cindy. So I left and went to my apartment.

Mind you, Sharon never cared before where I took Cindy. All that mattered was that I got her out of the house. It didn't matter the season or what the weather was like as long as I got Cindy out of her hair. Since the custody battle came up and after her mother-in-law told her she needed to be a mother to her child, Sharon became very concerned and was playing "Mommy catch up."

Now according to what Connor and Sharon explained to me, when Connor saw Sharon that evening, he told her he was happy to see Cindy at his office. "How so?" Sharon asked him. And he went on to tell her how Cindy and I dropped by the office to see him that afternoon.

Around 10:30 p.m., while relaxing, Sharon called. "Carol, how come you didn't tell me you took Cindy to Connor's office?"

"Oh, yeah, Connor asked me to bring Cindy over to say hello."

"I'm her mother. Don't you ever do something like that again."

"But you all live in the same house, and that's her father, who had asked me to stop by. But I apologize if you feel offended by not asking your permission after her father had asked me to drop by. You need to speak to your husband about this. Again, I'm sorry if this upset you."

I treated both of them with respect even though Sharon was so evil and bitter toward me. At the end of the day, it's a job, and I tried very hard not to take it too personal.

Another time Sharon stood in the family room and said, "I make all executive decisions in this house. And I don't care about Connor. All I care about is Cindy and Charlie."

Later on that night, Sharon started a thread of harassment. Every night, she texted me. It didn't matter the time, and it was always the same text, *I'm her mother and you are the nanny. You are the hired help. Don't forget that. I make all the decisions.*

The first night she texted me this, I texted her back, "I'm glad you've come to realize that you are the one who gave birth to her. For a while, I thought you had forgotten." She continued texting me, and I had to tell her, "I'm a grown woman" and do not appreciate her harsh and nasty remarks. After that, I decided not to engage with the back and forth texting because it had become obvious that Sharon was envious of the relationship I had with her daughter.

CHAPTER SIX

Betrayal

I DID NOT go to a university, but it doesn't take a rocket scientist to figure out that something was definitely wrong with Sharon. For Cindy's well being and stability, Sharon needed help and fast.

Soon after her harassing texts started, I saw Cindy at the house. She looked at me and said, "How many days are you here?" I was stunned when she asked me that. Apparently, she overheard Sharon talking, and it didn't take long for little Cindy to take notice.

I said, "Why did you ask?"

"I miss you, and I don't see you enough."

"I miss you too, but you need to spend more time together with your mommy."

Cindy bent her head, and tears started to run down her cheeks.

"Don't cry, Sweetheart. You'll still see me. And we can still have a wonderful time together, but a mother and daughter need to spend time alone."

To distract her I said, "Hey, let's read your favorite book."

She looked at me with a deep stare and smiled.

"Hey, what's that smile about?"

"I'm smiling because I love you."

Even though Sharon gave me a letter of termination, I realized that was just for show so the lawyers could see she doesn't have a nanny and she was the one caring for Cindy. I still had to pick Cindy up from camp, prepare her meals, do her laundry, but the only difference was both parents had to spend parenting time and make records for the courts.

Connor asked me not to leave because ninety percent of the time, she used to spend it with me, and the new adjustment would screw up his child's mental stability, and he didn't want Cindy to be like her mother, seeing a shrink all her life. He wanted her in a stable environment.

Sharon used to shop lavishly, and she made sure her parents were well taken care of. She had Connor pay for their health insurance, and she even bought them a house with all the furnishings using Connor's money.

The month she purchased the home for her parents was the first time I've ever seen her show affection for Connor. Sharon walked him to the door and kissed him, telling him she loved him, and he was sucked into her deceit and charm. Four months after the closing of her parent's home, she filed for divorce. She didn't even wait for the ink to dry. How clever!

Sharon became even more busy after that. She went traveling and hanging out more, going out with her new friends, including the decorator. I hardly saw much of Sharon at that time. She was busy putting things in place, and because of her being so busy, I felt like an unchained prisoner. The thing about Sharon was she was never without a nanny. The days I had off work, she made sure she had coverage from different nanny agencies.

Sharon claimed she could not stay in the marriage because Connor was very boring, and all he liked to do was watch *CSI* and a bunch of other television series, and that he was always on the computer; therefore, she couldn't stand to look at him. So, I guess to get back at him she spent his money. She spent a lot of time remodeling the house, buying new furniture, then she'd sell them and buy more. She also kept on hiring and then firing interior decorators because each one never did it right. She even went to Paris to buy furniture, yet none of that furniture worked. Each one of the decorators told her there was too much furniture, and they didn't even match. Moving trucks were always in and out taking out furniture. One day, I asked her where all the furniture was going. She replied, "I have a store now!" And she laughed out loud.

Sharon was very bubbly and happy, carrying out her plans as if it were revenge. She was nice as long as she got her way, and if you are having a conversation with her, you better filter your thoughts and analyze properly before you delivered an answer to her. She could be fun to hang out with, but if you give her any type of constructive criticism, she would turn into the little girl, Regan, from *The Exorcist*, possessed by the devil. Sharon had a free and vulgar mouth that slipped frequently.

So now that the divorce was at the boiling point Sharon was getting frustrated by the second. She was still living in the house, in separate bedrooms, of course. She had leased a house in the next town not too far away, but Connor would not allow her to take Cindy until the divorce was final.

Sharon and I were sitting outside one day when she said, "If Connor thinks he's going to keep me captive in this house, then I'll make his life miserable."

I asked her, "What about the house you leased?"

"I'm committed to pay for the house occupied or not."

At first, I didn't quite understand what she meant by making his life miserable until the next day when she told me she was running out, and she wanted me to stick around because she doesn't like how Connor cuddles Cindy.

"What!" I said.

"Nothing, nothing," she replied.

What is this woman up to now, I thought to myself.

I remember one time while I was on vacation Sharon called me. Now mind you, I was four to five thousand miles away from the USA, yet she wanted me to get on the next flight out to come back to work because she could not find a sitter and Cindy was not feeling well. Now, I had gone to visit my mother who had been rushed to the hospital very ill. I had no intention of cutting my vacation short, so I ignored her calls. When I returned to the States, Sharon was pissed and hardly spoke to me.

Another time Sharon flew to Miami for a business trip, she claimed. Before she left she arranged for me to meet with her mother, Jill. I called Sharon's mother several times but could not reach her. I even left several voice messages. I kept calling until she finally answered, and this was what she said to me.

"Where are you?"

"I'm on my way to meet you. I'll see you at 2:00 p.m."

"Carol, Carol, where are you?"

"I'm in New Jersey. I'm leaving the house now. I left messages on your voicemail. Let me know exactly where you're going to be, and I'll meet you."

"What time are you going to be here?"

I sighed quietly. "Two p.m., Jill."

She then accused me of not calling her, and she told me that I'm supposed to meet up with her for 2:00 p.m.

"It's now 1:30 p.m. It will only take me twenty minutes to get there."

She continued, "So when are you going to get here?"

"The time I'm supposed to be there," I said.

By now, I was beginning to get pissed off, feeling like a broken record.

Jill was very upset with me and said, "Carol, you don't follow instructions."

"Jill, you need to clarify with Sharon please."

Jill didn't say goodbye. I just heard the phone hang up. How rude!

A few minutes later, my phone rang. It was Sharon. "Carol, where the hell are you?"

"I'm on my way to meet your mom at 2:00 p.m. as you asked."

"My mother is frantic. And what am I supposed to do about that?"

"Call your mother and tell her to relax. I'll be there before 2:00 p.m."

Sharon and her mother sounded alike so much, so you couldn't tell the difference. They both yelled and asked the same questions repeatedly. I continued driving, got on the freeway, and those two miserable fucks continued to blow up my phone with their damn calls. I simply ignored the phone calls because I had made myself clear that I was on my way, so why the hell did those two old battle axes keep bothering me? If I answered, then I'll be a glutton for punishment, and I had no intentions of doing that to myself. No job was worth that. Besides, I was driving with a young child in the backseat on the freeway, and I was not going to put the safety of us and other drivers in jeopardy just to answer the phone, especially for those two ungrateful bitches. To hell with that! Jill would see me when I get there. Those two crazy ass, manipulative control freaks can kiss my ass, especially after I overheard them speaking about how fed up they were with the previous housekeepers. Jill had said, "Why don't you just hire two Mexicans, who will work from dusk till dawn and don't need a lot of space in the house. And you can pay them whatever you want. They are not going to complain. They're just happy they're in America and have a roof over their heads."

I arrived at my destination at 1:55 p.m. By that time, Cindy was fast asleep. I guess not fun for Grandma Jill. That bitch was so cold to me. She didn't even say thank you for bringing her granddaughter to her. Hmm! Living with wealthy people may seem nice from the outside looking in; however, all that glitters is not gold. The talking down to, and the belittling was quite enough. But the carrying on as though I was an indentured servant, placing crazy demands such as don't say this, do this now, bring me some water, oh, I changed my mind, bring me juice instead, oh, no, you put it in the wrong glass, made me feel like this was fucking hell on Earth.

CHAPTER SEVEN

Connor's Confession

CONNOR SAID HE thought that he had met the woman of his dreams, and divorce was never in the cards. "I never cheated on Sharon. Sharon made me do things that I strictly forbid," he said to me.

"What did you do Connor?"

"Well, she introduced me to marijuana and Coke."

"Wow! Did you try it? And how did it make you feel?"

"I hated it, but I watched her sniff the Coke and smoke the weed. She got high, and we'd have crazy sex."

I've never heard Connor talk like that. I'm still in shock up to this day.

Connor continued, "Sharon loves food. Weed will do that to you. But staying skinny was her top priority. She'd smoke and head straight to the kitchen, eat up anything she put her hands on, and immediately after she'd head back upstairs with a spoon, lean over the toilet bowl, and bring all the food back up until her stomach was empty."

Oh, my! No wonder she had so much stomach pains.

I can't understand why an intelligent man would allow another person to lead him down that path, knowing the consequences of drugs. I guess pussy rules the world, and boy, Connor was pussy whipped by Sharon.

In the back of my mind, I knew this relationship was not normal. I noticed when Sharon would speak to Connor she spoke to him like a parent scolding a child, and he would bend his head down and answer, "Okay, Sharon. Whatever you want," or, "Whatever makes you happy. Can I leave the room now, Sharon?"

"No, I'm still speaking to you. You'll leave when I tell you to."

Connor would bend his head and whispers, "Okay."

What the fuck was that! This was the twenty first century, and Sharon was mentally abusing Connor. She always reminded him of his birth defects. He was born with his hands and feet webbed, and doctors had to do several operations to try to make it look as normal, but it was very noticeable to the eyes. He was in constant pain and took medication to help make it through the day. He was very humble and never complained. He just focused on his business, and the more money he made sex with Sharon was A-okay, and Connor would be happy.

Nothing else or no one mattered, not even his relatives. He would tell me not to speak to his family because he was concerned about the flow of information. In the eyes of Connor's relatives, he was their rich hero. His entire family benefited from Connor's wealth. After all, he is the owner of two professional sports teams, three companies, a fleet of real estate properties, and a fleet of cars. They all looked up to Connor as he bragged and gave them advice.

Deep down, none of his relatives knew how unhappy and miserable his marriage was to Sharon. As long as the money flowed, Sharon was living it up, doing her own thing. And then that dreaded day occurred—the stock market crashed. Connor lost three quarters of his wealth. Over fifty million dollars. That day, Sharon yelled out like Tarzan, King of the Jungle. She started yelling at him, "You are stupid! You fucking retard! I want out of this marriage, and I'll take you for everything else that's left!"

I told myself maybe I should quit now, but how could I leave Cindy. Sharon's parental skills were so screwed up, and Connor was running a business. I felt stuck. I didn't want to abandon Cindy and especially with all the allegations that Sharon started plotting. I feared that Connor would be accused of child molestation. That was Sharon's way of getting full custody and getting a big piece of the pie.

I have seen and heard of the most sickening parental skills of all times living in that home.

Sharon's choices of words were inappropriate for a child. She started telling Cindy that her inner thighs, close to her vagina was called sweet meat, and she would tickle her there constantly. When it was Cindy's bedtime, Sharon would tell her, "Go to your room and do private things." By then, Cindy was old enough to understand her mother very well. Cindy would obey and get under the covers, and she would start moaning, turning her face from side to side with her mouth open. I soon realized she was masturbating. I caught her doing it many times, and

I asked Sharon what the hell was going on. Why is Cindy pleasuring herself at such a tender age? My god, she was only three and a half years old.

Sharon replied, "It's okay for her to do that as long as she does it privately."

"Says who?"

"Oh! I mentioned it to her doctor, and the doctor said it's okay."

At the time, I told myself, *they are rich, and I'm only the nanny. Who the hell is going to listen to me?* But what blew me away was when I walked into Cindy's bathroom while she was taking a bath, and Sharon stood by the door clapping her hands and singing a really strange song.

"Penis in the butt, penis in the butt, penis in the butt."

She and Cindy were singing the song together, and when I walked in the room, Sharon stopped singing and just began laughing. Now, I'm telling myself, *this is not a damn song any parent should be teaching a child. What the hell is Sharon up to? Oh, I get it!* The pieces of the puzzle fitted perfectly. A few days ago, Sharon told me to keep an eye on Connor. She did not want me to leave Cindy alone with him. She didn't like how he cuddled with her under the bed sheets and to make sure the door was always open to my view. By this time, Cindy knew her parents were getting a divorce, and she started acting out by slamming doors and biting herself, so she started seeing a child psychologist. I also started feeling pressured and called Connor's sister, Jessica, and told her of the madness that was going on in the house.

A couple of days later, Connor said he wanted to speak with me. He said I had to protect Cindy and him. He asked that I make a full report of all my observations and speak to his lawyers. Now, I was scared and started going down memory lane. After all, Sharon was nutty. I agree, but I started remembering the good times and laughter I shared with Sharon. Then I recalled watching her tricks with Connor, and I really didn't care. I was just the nanny/house manager. I told him, "If I did that, Sharon will be pissed, so you'll have to guarantee me that my job is secured." Connor said, "Don't worry. You have your job here with Cindy and me until she turns eighteen years. "Really," I said to myself, "okay."

CHAPTER EIGHT

Seductive and Clever

WHENEVER SHARON WANTED Connor to give her big cash, she was so clever and cunning about it. I remembered one day she went bike riding. She had just bought this new bike and wanted to try it out. It was one of those racing bike with a skinny seat that you're supposed to wear padded racer pants with, but apparently, Sharon didn't buy one yet, but still, she took the bike out for a spin.

She came home from bike riding, dropped the bike, walked with her legs wide open while holding her crotch saying, "That bike just fucked up my vagina."

I just burst out in laughter. I said, "What happened?"

She explained of not having the padded pants hurt her. Then she went through the house calling out to Connor.

"Connor! My vagina will not be good later, so come and take care of business now because later it's going to be sore."

Connor was so happy to get a little fix since he didn't get much, according to Sharon. After her fun, Connor fell asleep. Sharon came downstairs telling me, "I fucked him, and he's sleeping like a baby."

The next day, Connor came downstairs and said to Sharon, "You wanted some money, so I just transferred $100,000.00 in your account."

Sharon was always trying so hard to start a business as part of her escape plan, but every time she tried, for some reason, it never worked out. She tried cosmetics and fashion but neither worked. One day she told me, "My husband is so fucking rich to have this problem."

Clever Sharon decided to go into the furniture business. She used the credit card that Connor provided and bought furniture. Connor never questioned the credit card bills because her job was to redecorate the mansion. She would sell the furniture for double the price and stash the money in a secret bank account. Connor controlled the finances, but his assistant paid all the bills, and he gave Sharon shopping allowances whenever she wanted. But that was not enough for Sharon. After all, her husband was a multimillionaire, and they both were like crabs in a bucket, trying to control each other.

I too travelled across country to another state with her to help her pick out furniture, not knowing what she was up to at the time. She called up her contacts, and the furniture was shipped directly to the recipient.

I have never met anyone in my entire life so fake, two faced, selfish, bold, and pompous. It seemed as though power and authority was of great importance to Sharon since growing up she was never allowed to make suggestions in her mother's house. Now she was in control of a powerful man and his finances and was drunk on power. To quote Lord Acton, "Power tends to corrupt and absolute power corrupts absolutely."

Sharon had a weird behavior of calling me a bitch sometimes. I ignored all her name calling and told myself it was just a job. Just because a person has money does not mean they are better than a person who has very little money. And that does not give the one with the money the right to talk down to or insult one's integrity. I've worked for a couple of millionaires and one billionaire in my time as a nanny and never had to work in such an environment. The billionaire and his family I worked for always showed me great respect.

Taking care of children is priceless, especially when you have a loyal, trustworthy, mother-like figure as a caregiver. I've worked for a very popular comedian as a nanny for his children. And my observation was, on stage, his personality was that of a hilarious yet reckless man with a nasty mouth. However, at home, he was humble, a great father, and a really wonderful human being. He was like night and day. He respected people, and that was important. A lot of people don't practice respecting each other, and when you don't show respect, then whatever you sow ye shall reap.

There's nothing wrong with enhancing your body to look and feel better about yourself, but some women do it for ulterior motives. They use their body to catch men, especially rich men. They don't even care if he is not their type. The money in the man's pocket makes him look mighty fine. But as the saying goes, "Money doesn't run after the woman." It's the other way around. Pussy can make a king lose his throne and his dignity. Sharon knew this because not only did she keep her body right, but she became best of friends with her Botox doctor.

To me, all of this was just vanity. I don't understand why some women would do such a thing. It's just another form of prostitution. They use their bodies as bait, and the weak minded man will be drawn to it. I heard a man say one time, "If you're not gay, then pussy rules the world. A man can't help the temptation when he sees a fine piece of ass."

When a man gives away his fortune and turns away from his family for that piece of ass, you know he is pussy whipped. As a mother of two grown men, I pray to God that they don't fall into the trap of a gold digger. A gold digger has one aim, and that's *the money*. They are so cunning and calm, and believe me. I knew I was in the presence of a gold digger after watching Sharon. She'll get on the phone with Connor and speak to him in a very nice tone just to get her way, and after the phone call ended, she'd turn to me and say, "How am I doing?" And I'd say, "You're good. You're damn good." And she would smile and say, "He's so retarded."

Connor was an amazing man. I've never seen him angry, or I never heard him yell at Sharon. Whatever she said he agreed to. The authority he gave her made her feel powerful. Some people don't know the difference between Dear Friend and Dear Fool. Connor seemed to be a genuine dear friend, but go tell Sharon that and she would not believe it. After all, she knows him and knows how he can trick people just as he would at card games in the casino.

Sharon was soon going out of her mind because she wanted to move out of the house, but she didn't want to leave without Cindy. With the legal proceedings over the custody battle and without her child, the meal ticket, she had too much to lose, so she was making everyone around her very miserable, even his parents. Well, now she was showing her true colors. She wanted no more communication with them. I had the pleasure of spending a week at their home out of state while the divorce was taking place. They were very heart broken. They cried every day while I was there, and all they kept on saying was, "She is part of our family. We love her. Maybe she needs medicine to help calm her down so she'll think straight. Maybe she should go see another psychiatrist because people don't just wake up and flip out like that." To me, they were in denial because they never lived with her. Years ago, Sharon told me of her intentions, but because of Connor's parents' medical history of heart attacks, strokes, and cancer, I could not relay all of these to them. But they had a pretty good idea of what was going on at the time and so far up to when I left their home, they were handling it and trying to come to terms with Connor and Sharon's divorce. I think crying and having family support really did help. Most of the family members were at Connor's parent's house for that week. It was sad at times but bittersweet to see the family come together. We all went out to dinner and didn't talk about the divorce that evening. At sundown, Connor's mother prayed. I listened to her praying. She was so amazing. She prayed for every family member by name including Sharon, and she wished everyone well.

You know the history of mothers-in-law, and we have a bad stain on us. They say mothers-in-law don't like daughters-in-law. Well, that's not always true. We love our daughters-in-law, but it can be conditional. After all, blood is thicker than water, but at the same time, you have to be fair especially if it concerns a long term relationship. Logically speaking, the best way is to stay out of the drama and let them work their own shit out.

CHAPTER NINE

House of Horrors

NOW THAT CONNOR and Sharon were sleeping in separate bedrooms, Sharon would lock her bedroom door, but Connor's bedroom had no lock so that Sharon would walk into Connor's room as she well damned pleased. No knocking. Oh, no! She did not need Connor's permission, but on the other hand, Connor could not do the same. Connor called in a locksmith to put a combination lock and asked me to assist the locksmith since he had a meeting.

Sharon heard the drilling and yelled out, "What the hell is going on here?"

I replied, "Connor is having the locksmith put a lock on his bedroom door."

Sharon walked up the stairs saying, "Carol, you think I don't know what is going on? I hope you have a good retirement plan. Look at you! You feel you are the queen bee looking over everything that's going on here. I made sure you got paid on time, and I made sure you didn't get taken advantage of."

"Really, Sharon! I'm only following instructions."

Sharon started saying, "I don't want you in my fucking house. I'm calling the police to put you out of my house."

Now I'm confused, and the locksmith was in shock. He called Connor. Connor told him to ignore her and finish up the job. I then texted Connor. "Please come home ASAP."

He texted me back saying he picked Cindy up and took her for ice cream and that he'll be home in five minutes. When he arrived home, more drama continued.

Cindy started screaming. Connor asked that I keep Cindy out of the house while he tried to make peace with Sharon. The yelling from Sharon had everyone in the house startled and scared. All of the house staff was asked to leave and take the rest of the week off.

Sharon was yelling at Connor, telling him she didn't clear out her closet and still had personal effects in the master bedroom. Connor told her the door wasn't locked as of yet, so get busy. Sharon grabbed some bags and started packing her stuff. All the time, the locksmith was doing his work. He turned to me and said, "She's a real bitch." He was pissed. Connor then told her when the locksmith was done, the door will be locked.

Sharon told Connor she owned half of the house, and she could do whatever she damn well pleased. Sharon called her lawyer and complained to the lawyer. Her lawyer advised her, but Sharon was yelling at the lawyer. I could tell Sharon was not happy with the lawyer's advice. Connor asked Sharon, "Let me talk to your lawyer."

"Go talk to your own damn lawyer."

Then she turned to him. "I'll get a fucking court order to get the rest of my things out of the master bedroom."

She also said she'll make sure he didn't get her daughter and that he'll have the fight of his life.

She told me, "Remember, he has a heart condition."

Connor looked and acted very fearful of Sharon because he would start saying okay to her and sit there while she carried on. He would look very pale, and he would stay silent and stop engaging in the argument. When he didn't answer her, that pissed her off, and her entire demeanor would change. Her eyeballs looked like they were popping out, and she would yell even more using profound language that would make a sailor blush. Connor would just sit there ignoring her. She would then start running up and down the stairs slamming doors, rearranging furniture and yelling at the dog because he barked too much.

This job turned into the worst job I've ever done in my life. By this time, the only reason for me staying on the job was little Cindy. Connor begged me not to leave, so I continued to go to work not knowing what to expect from Sharon. She was like a ticking time bomb. I could not believe this was the same person who had a meeting with one of the housekeepers and tell us she wanted both of us to continue to work for her after the divorce. This woman was insane. How could you terminate someone and still give them orders and instructions. Unbelievable!

Two weeks before Sharon moved out of the home, I got a phone call from the housekeeper. She was crying. I asked what was wrong, and she told me Sharon just terminated her. I advised her to call Connor. He told the housekeeper Sharon does not pay her, so she needed to come to work as usual. That pissed Sharon off that she now had no authority over the staff. But out of respect, when we went to work, we still said good morning to Sharon. She would give everyone the evil eye, and she'll answer in a sharp tone. From the time I worked for the Goldsteins, Sharon terminated eight housekeepers. Mind you, they were good at their job and were fired for no reason.

The next day, Connor asked me to buy some groceries and prepare some meals for the week. On my arrival at work, Sharon came into the kitchen and told me, "You can pack away the groceries, but please leave my fucking house." I said, "Okay" and didn't even bother to put the groceries away. I just went straight out the door put the bags in my car and left. I texted Connor, and he said to prepare the meals in my home and drop them off around six that evening; by then, he would be home, and Sharon may quiet down. It was so bizarre when I arrived at work. Sharon would help herself to the dinner that I prepared. Was she for real? No one would believe the hell she put me through. As long as Connor was at home, she had very little to say to me. She mostly gave me instructions about the house, and she would compliment me on how delicious the food tasted. But when Connor was not at home, all hell would break loose, and she'd become a total bitch from the minute I walked through that door. She would start slamming doors and open drawers then slamming them shut as she pretended to look for something she could not find. She would yell at me, saying this and that was missing and accusing me of not doing things the way she wanted it. She ordered me to put the pantry in alphabetical order and labeled. She continued to snap, insult, degrade me, and remind me that she was the one who gave birth to Cindy. I told Connor about her behavior, and when he confronted Sharon about it, she denied everything. It bothered me because it's was her word against mine. I started to feel so stressed out that I started to get headaches on a daily basis. The mental abuse from Sharon was really driving me up a wall. But, I continued to bite my tongue and not lose my cool. I didn't want to have an outburst because I realized she's trying her best to tantalize me, but I am smarter than that. I knew it was a trap, and I ain't a small time homie from the West Indies. And yet, I was brought up to respect people's home. However, that does not mean to say I am a pushover, and even though I don't use obscene language does not mean I don't know how to use it in the right context, and it would be Caribbean style, so she would be made to feel small.

When Sharon would start flapping her lips, in my mind, I would curse her out. *What the fuck is wrong with you woman! Why don't you shut the fuck up! Every mother fucking time I come in here, you always have something to say to me. You ain't my boss no more. You don't pay me. Enough is enough. FUCK!*

But, as I said, I grew up different and in a Christian home.

Sharon would continue to run her mouth oblivious to the fact that her flapping mouth had no effect on the staff's paychecks. Still she harassed me and all who worked in the house. Her plans were to make sure she aggravated everyone so that they'll be so frustrated they would leave. But I was her main target.

The weekend came, and Connor had to take Cindy to his sister's to spend time with her cousins. And on Sunday afternoon, I got a call from Connor. "Can you please come to the house?" He sounded very hysterical.

"What happened? Is Cindy okay?"

"Yes she's fine. Please come."

I walked in the house, and Connor looked at me in disbelief. Sharon raped the house of all the expensive furniture. It was jaw dropping. Connor was shaking. Sharon was a very clever woman. She waited until Connor left the house with Cindy knowing he wouldn't be back until Sunday night to do her deed. But that wasn't all. Sharon made sure she put her clothes in every closet in the house and left it there so that she had an excuse to come back and have free access to the house. Sharon told Connor he cannot change the locks in the house even if she moved out because everything was 50/50 right down the middle.

Connor called Sharon and told her she has one week to get all her personal belongings. The next day, Connor called the locksmith and had him change all the locks in the house. He had the staff pack up all of Sharon's belongings and place them in the garage. And Connor filed a motion with the court for Sharon to give him twenty-four hours' notice to enable her to pick up her belongings. Connor instructed the staff not to allow Sharon back in the house, not even to use the bathroom.

When Sharon came to the house, she was bitter, going out of her mind when she rang the doorbell, and the housekeeper spoke to her from the intercom, telling her she had instructions not to allow her in the house. This made Sharon furious. She started rooting out the plants and throwing them on the walkway. Then she started cussing, "Who the fuck do you people think I am? This is my fucking house, and I'll make sure to sell it and put all of you people out of work."

The housekeeper told her, "Ms. Goldstein, if you cannot contain yourself, I will have no choice but to call the police."

Sharon just got in her Bentley and drove off.

Connor's lawyers filed a protective order against Sharon, and it was ordered by the court. Sharon was so pissed at her own lawyer for not doing enough.

I was subpoenaed to come to court to give valuable evidence pertaining to the custody of Cindy; however, Sharon and her lawyer got in a dispute and Sharon fired her so that subpoena got cancelled. Sharon hired a new law firm to represent her at the expense of Connor. The legal fees kept piling up, and Connor and Sharon were at war because not only did he have to pay for his own legal fees he had to pay for Sharon's as well. In the weeks ahead, I noticed that Sharon simmered down a little. She had taken a different approach since the mediator for the minor child, Cindy's lawyer, made recommendations as to who will have custody. Cindy's lawyer told Sharon she needed to be civil and cordial or she would have no choice but to recommend that Cindy live with her father because her arrogant attitude and behavior was making her look very bad. So she didn't have a choice but to listen to the lawyers. This, for Sharon, was not a normal way of life. She had lost so much weight; she looked scary and acted as an old lady nitpicking at every little thing.

One day, Sharon called me. She was crying and sobbing on the phone. "Carol, I miss my dog, and I don't know what I'm going to do without my dog."

"This is none of my concern. You need to speak to Connor about this. I am very busy. Have yourself a blessed day. Goodbye."

The woman had lost her mind. Connor told me Sharon hired another attorney to represent Charlie, yup, the dog, to determine custody. Are you kidding me! Who the fuck hires an attorney for a pet? What happened to the law firm Sharon hired? This was getting interesting by the minute.

The money Sharon was stashing away, well, some of it was recovered and got frozen toward community property. When Sharon found out about the money she stashed away, she got even more devious and bitchy toward me. Before Sharon filed for divorce, she told me it would be smooth sailing because Connor was retarded. Never in her wildest dreams did she think he would put up a fight. At the house where I continued to work along with the same staff, working conditions had become less stressful since Sharon was no longer residing there. My hours were flexible and I had more time for myself, but everything is not final and soon will be short lived.

Now the in-laws were at war. Roberta called Jill and asked that she please speak to her daughter, Sharon, because she was causing stress on Connor and his business. Jill told Roberta to mind her own business. Roberta told Jill that Connor is her business. Jill then told Roberta that she's an old sick woman with cancer. They had a yelling match over the phone. Now they were not speaking to each other.

Sharon was very busy sending emails to Connor, complaining to the lawyers and child psychologists. She would complain about everything that came across her mischievous brain. She was performing her witch bitch roll very well. She became very desperate. She called Connor's father so he could speak to Roberta to apologize for being so nasty to her mom, Jill. Connor's dad said, "Sharon, I'm not supposed to talk to you. Goodbye," and hung up the phone. Connor's dad was Sharon's drinking buddy. Now both families were bitter enemies.

CHAPTER TEN

Walking on Eggshells

THE LAST TIME I saw Sharon, she looked ten years older. She looked like Cindy's grandmother. Her deeds were catching up with her. Everything I told Sharon about divorce and the effects it would have on Cindy was happening and all at once. The outbursts of screaming, staring in the windows, and sitting in the closet were the behaviors Cindy was displaying. She looked spaced out, and she asked a lot of questions. She was confused and could not understand why her parents were living in separate homes and why she had to go back and forth.

One weekend, when Connor picked Cindy up from Sharon's new home, Cindy asked me, "Is my mom and dad mad at me?"

"No, not at all. They just like different things and decided to live in separate homes, but it has absolutely nothing to do with you."

To my amazement, Cindy said, "I hope those two can get along and stop the stupid arguing."

This divorce was long and dragging because of the greed, and even though Sharon no longer lived at the house, she still controlled Connor to a certain extent especially when the parenting issues come up. Sharon would email Connor, don't do this, don't do that, instructions on how to feed Cindy, the time for her bath and bed, what we are allowed to say to her, how to pack her lunch—basically things she never did before. And of course, all the emails were in copy to the mediator and child psychologist. She was just nitpicking at every little shit. If Connor was one minute late to pick Cindy up, she'd call her lawyer. If he was fifteen minutes too early and Sharon would run out of her house and wave the court order documents in his face. Connor said to her, "I know I'm early, so take your time." Sharon objects and tells him to leave her property and return on the hour.

Dealing with Sharon, you are definitely walking on eggshells or rather like having splinters in your feet. Just the thought that Connor lost a lot of money in his investments didn't sit right with Sharon. She constantly called him retarded. This divorce became very nasty with bitterness and greed. Connor lost so much money, so whatever remained, he started to hide his money and funneling the cash through friends and other investments. This was the first time Connor ever stood up for himself and finally started wearing the pants or so you would think.

He realized now that Sharon used him, took him for granted, betrayed him, deceived him, and hurt and humiliated him. When Connor's dad, Connery, heard that Sharon cheated on Connor with a black man he shouted, "**Sharon is a mother fucking Hitler! And I will get a hit man to fuck her up!**"

I remembered Sharon telling me she would leave Connor about a year after we moved from the city but thought she was joking as she always did, so I blew it off and didn't pay no attention even though she didn't laugh when she was saying it but she had a perfect plan. I did not anticipate that she would actually carry it out. Sharon also told me, "The divorce will be so easy because the man loves me, and he will agree with whatever I tell him to do."

I remember saying to her, "I hope the divorce don't end up like the war of the roses."

She replied, "Not at all." She was so sure of herself.

The custody before the final separation was just a temporary arrangement to co-parent to see if the arrangement could work. And Sharon made sure she did everything in her power to prove he was an unfit father. Sharon continued to undermine Connor's parenting time. All of a sudden, nothing he did can please Sharon. She was fighting for all that she can get down to the last straw.

She was acting extremely desperate and curvaceous. Connor tried to ignore her and asked me to do the same. They continued to fight. Whenever Sharon saw me, she would start acting all pompous, and she would drop nasty remarks at me.

Sharon walked around with an air of confidence, and why? Because Connor had no pre-nup. This was the first sign of a gold digger. She had refused to sign it. Connor did mention to Sharon if she would sign a pre-nup, and she said, "Of course, no problem." Connor was so in love that he didn't press the issue. After they got married, Connor asked his lawyer to come to the house with the post-nup documents, and Connor told her to sign it. Connor was in shock when Sharon told him, "I'm not signing no fucking post-nup." Now this was a big red flag and one of Connor's biggest mistakes. This is a learning lesson for all those well-to-do men or women whose partner refuses to sign a premarital or postnuptial agreement. It just goes to show, "Intent is in the eyes of a gold digger."

CHAPTER ELEVEN

Trouble and Confusion

IN THE EARLIER days, I did more than my share of duty. Sharon entertained and hosted a lot of parties at the house. One year, she celebrated her mom, Jill's, birthday. I decorated the cake and helped prepared the food. Two waitresses were hired to serve and clean up.

When the family started to arrive, Sharon introduced me to them, so I was shocked when the party started, and Sharon told me I was not allowed to sit at the dinner table with the guest. I asked why, and she said, "Carol, my mom won't sit at the table with the hired help."

"Oh I see." But in my mind, I was thinking, *who the fuck does she think she is with her pulled up face always looking surprised all the time.* Boy, did I feel like an alien or was it discrimination or racism? I was very insulted. I left the main dining room and went to my room and watched TV. I did not come back out for the night.

Connor's parents were much easier to get along with. They were very loving and down to earth, and they made sure I was very comfortable. Never once did I feel rejected or felt like hired help when I was with Connor's family. But, those were the days.

Sharon was having issue after issue. She accused him of not being a good father. She would put potting soil in Cindy's lunch box and dump dirty laundry in plastic bags, which she would keep for three weeks, so by the time she sent it back, you had no choice but to dump it. Sharon would keep all the nice cute clothes and send her back to her father in clothes a few sizes smaller so that he would be forced to buy new clothes. Once, she sent a baby size sock with an adult sized sock just to piss him off. This woman did all kinds of crazy, clever things just to manipulate him. After doing this madness, Sharon sent an email to the mediator and the child psychologist telling them all the things she did he in fact did them and that it was not in the best interest of the child for her to live with her father. This was all part of her master plan, just making up lies. Sharon even tried to put Cindy against her father by telling Cindy that her daddy put them out of the house. She insisted that as part of their agreement, Connor must have life insurance and put her as the beneficiary.

Days and weeks went by, and I started waking up at nights. My heart was pounding so hard as if it was coming out of my chest. I started having regular headaches and sleepless nights.

I keep remembering the conversation Sharon and I had. *Is she for real?* Sharon said the lawyers were going to question me, and she was concerned as to what I was going to say. Sharon used to volunteer information about her marriage and the reasons for the break up. I told Sharon I knew they had problems, and I preferred not to get involved.

"Well, Carol, you're here most of the time, and the lawyers won't question a stranger. I will do whatever it takes to make sure that Connor does not get custody of my child."

"If the lawyers want to question me, I will have no choice but to speak the truth of my observations while living and working for the both of you."

"Carol! You're not listening to me!"

"I am. But you're telling me things I've never seen to tell the lawyers, and I don't think I can do what you are telling me."

"Carol, after the divorce, I will get a lot of cash, and I will buy a house, and you can move in with Cindy and me. I'll give you your own section of the house to live so that you can continue to care for Cindy."

My thoughts were, *is she trying to bribe me? Who the fuck does she think she is?*

The next day, Cindy and I were in the playroom, and all of a sudden, Cindy started crying.

"Why are you crying Cindy?"

"My mom and dad are getting a divorce," she said as she sobbed harder.

"Even though they are getting a divorce, their love for you will never change. Do you hear me. That will never change!"

"Okay," she said trying to control her tears.

"Just because they don't like sleeping in the same bed no more does not mean they don't love you. Don't be sad, Sweetie. Everything will be alright."

Then Cindy said something that really broke my heart. "Are you going to divorce me too?"

"No! That's for married people."

"Then promise me. Promise me you never leave me."

"I promise you. You have my word. I love you too much to go away and not be with you. Cindy, you know you can tell me anything that's bothering you. I am your friend, and I'll make sure to protect you. I love you like my own family."

"I know you love me, but I don't know why my mommy loves me to sing that song."

"That's a silly song, and if you don't know why she likes it, then you need to ask your mom."

"But, Carol, boys have penises and girls have vaginas."

"Yup! And that's why we don't sing about private parts of the body. It's private!"

"I don't know why the heck those two don't get along," Cindy said.

Wow! That kid was very smart! She spoke like a nine or ten year old.

Sharon never liked the idea of being a 24/7 mom, and for some reason, she resented Cindy, saying, "That kid is so fucking ugly and too fat, and she cries too much." I realized then that no mother in their right mind would say that about the child she gives birth to. I realized too that Sharon must be a really sick woman. No wonder why Connor called me one day and told me to be careful of how I speak to Sharon and that if there was anything I wanted to talk about I should run it by him first. Hmmm! Interesting!

I knew that she was on heavy medication, and sometimes, she could not even get out of bed. I would drive her to her doctor's appointments, and she would tell me, "I don't know what I'll do without you." Yeah right! Deep down in my gut, I knew that it was a regular fake statements that employers use. But if you take too much days off or reach to work late, you'll see just how much they love you then. That's the conditional love I was talking about. They love you for what you can do for them. I know because I've experienced it with this job.

When Sharon filed for divorce, we were still friends. And when I decided not to go along with her lies, that bitch became very cold toward me. She called me aside and said, "Carol, I don't need your services." But I already knew she was going to do that because Connor had warned me. Luckily for me, I had my own apartment by then.

Months passed and the divorce proceedings were well on going. Finally, that dreaded day arrived. The doorbell rang at my apartment. I peeked through the window and saw a man with some documents standing there. The man very apologetically served me with a subpoena. The subpoena got cancelled but that was short lived. A couple of months later, I was served another subpoena, which got cancelled as well. I was so saddened by this amount of drama. My life was not the same, and finally, I thought maybe it was time to leave the job, but Connor begged me not to. He said not to worry, that he had my back, and I must have his. "I know it's a lot for you to consume. Welcome to my life," Connor told me. He added, "You cannot crumble on me now."

Prior to me getting subpoenaed, Sharon moved into her new house, but our nightmare just began. Connor had to pay for all the legal fees because she didn't work. The stress of the back and forth bickering trickled down to everyone in the house including his sisters and parents.

All the family members were interviewed by a psychologist. One by one, we went into a room, and we all had a sad face. I can't believe one human being can affect so many lives. Even close friends had to give a statement or character report about Sharon and Connor. Sharon's character report was astonishing, and now Connor realized that he married one of the worst tramps in the history of the world. Someone Sharon knew very well gave a character statement, and I was shocked. The ex friend of Sharon said, she would befriend her girlfriend's husband while she lived in Miami, and then out of the blue, Sharon would say, "Don't you know I'm fucking your husband?" One man she dated faked a terminal illness to break up with her. The thing was once you date her, you cannot get away that easily. She admitted to me that she was a stalker.

CHAPTER TWELVE

The Root of All Evil

THREE LONG TAUNTING years have passed before another subpoena was served. I was starting to get accustomed to the mental abuse. I was so stressed out by all this madness. Connor had depositions every month and sometimes twice or three times a week, and he'll come home so aggravated that he would unzip his pants and just piss in all her favorite, expensive pots of plants that she had yet to pick up after the divorce was final. And, he would say aloud, "Fuck you, bitch."

Finally, the day for my deposition arrived. I walked in the room feeling uncomfortable already when one of the female lawyers said, "Here comes the star of the hour!" In my mind, I was thinking, *what the fuck is she talking about? You're putting me in the hot seat, and I'm the star?* It's like the rooster telling the turkey "Happy Thanksgiving!" Go figure. What a bitch!

I felt like I was the elephant in the room at the lawyers office, and they are talking and laughing, and I felt victimized. Sharon walked in the room and her eyes attempted to pierce mine, but you cannot pierce the truth because lies are covered by veils and curtains. I could see her anguish and bitterness toward me. I told her once that I was under oath you can kiss that pinkie swear goodbye. I had no intentions of purging myself to save her. That bitch was on her own. She could lie as much as she wanted. That's on her. The lawyers drilled me with questions. At one point, Sharon jumped out of her chair and ran out of the room. She came back in after a couple of minutes with blood red eyes, holding a cup of tea. Connor told me later, "I was scared and thought she would throw the tea at you." I had made it clear to her that I was not going to sin my soul with her lies.

This divorce was mentally draining for the entire family. And forget about the attorney fees, which was running a million dollars plus. Finally, Sharon decided to settle out of court. How clever. She didn't even want to go through my entire testimony for fear that she would lose custody because I really had her cornered. When Connor heard she wanted to settle, he was happy to have this madness over. Connor told me that I never had to worry about my job or money because I had his back and helped him get fifty percent custody of Cindy.

The agreement between Sharon and Connor was that Connor ceased to employ me on the days when Cindy was with Connor, but I was allowed to see her for a couple of hours a month. This was just a temporary arrangement. When I saw the agreement, Connor told me that Sharon had discriminated me and my family, and he thought I should sue her to get my name off of the divorce decree. I asked him, "How am I going to do that?" He then introduced me to someone who dealt with that kind of stuff, and I filed a lawsuit against Sharon. What the hell. She already hated my guts.

Connor told me he wanted me to crush Sharon to get my name off the decree so that things could get back to normal. "After all, Cindy misses you and cries for you," he said. I also missed her a lot. Cindy was a very smart kid, and she started putting the pieces together.

One morning, I was cooking eggs when Cindy came into the kitchen. She was staring around and looking spaced out.

"What's going on, Sweetie?" I asked her.

"Please tell me that story about the little kids you cared for a long time ago," she said as the tears started rolling down her cheeks.

I dropped to my knees and held her. I couldn't hold back my tears, then I dried my eyes quickly so that she couldn't see and I said, "Those kids are grown now, and I do see them from time to time."

"But I want to see you forever," Cindy said.

"You are going to see me just not every day. I want you to be brave, honest, polite, loving, caring, be kind to your friends and family, work hard in school, and aim for the stars. I want you to be successful. I also want you to practice playing the piano a little more. I know it's hard, but in life, you go through stages, and you're a big girl."

"People change from babies to children to teenagers and then you are all grown up. I know it's hard, but we all go through this in life. I can always be your friend, and I'm a phone call away."

Just then, Connor came downstairs and asked what was going on. I told him of the conversation I just had with Cindy, and he replied, "She'll get over it." I couldn't believe he just said that so casual. Damn! He could be so cold at times.

There was so much tension in that house that I couldn't concentrate. I was and still am mentally drained that I had to see a psychologist to help me put some sense to this madness because it really bothered me. I saw her almost every Wednesday because I was worried and stressed. I was worried about Cindy. Her mother was a nut case, and her father, even though he was a nice guy, could be insensitive at times. I worried about her mental state and what this divorce was doing to her. Her behavior had changed from a normal child to one of a troubled child. She would stare out the window, sit in the corner of her closet, and once, she told me she was scared of her mom because she liked to yell and doesn't allow her to finish saying her feeling. She told me, "Only you and my feelings doctor listens and daddy is always on the computer or watching sports on TV."

I know Cindy will be financially okay, but in her social life, I couldn't see it looking too bright. I feared that she would have trust issues with her parents and might even have mental issues.

Both parties are guilty of lying to their child, which is extremely bad moral ethics. I say this because they both told this child on more than one occasion that I was a part of her family. They allowed this child to bond with me and then to eliminate me out of her life without an explanation was cruel and can affect a child mentally.

You see, Sharon was scared that I would poison Cindy's mind and put her against her mother. But I was wiser than that. One day I'm sure, because she is smart, Cindy would put the pieces together. Anytime you file motions and lawsuits, which become public records and can be easily retrieved. Who are you kidding? It all boils down to money. It has become toxic!

Both parents continued to see a child psychologist, who, I was told, suggested that since I was suing Sharon should not be a part of Cindy's life because if she found out that someone was trying to hurt her mother, it could cause more mental damage on her. Therefore, I should be terminated and have no more further contact with Cindy. When I was told this, I could not stop the tears. I thought this was all a dream. Connor was sobbing and clapping and hitting the table when he told me.

"I don't want you to go job hunting," he said to me. "I'll take care of you. Do you hear me? Look into my eyes, Carol. Do you hear me?"

"Yes, thank you," was all I could reply.

"Now, this is what I want you to do for me. I want you to make dinner for the three of us, and we'll have a going away celebration for you. I want you to tell a lie to Cindy. Tell her that you are going back to the Caribbean to take care of your mother and that you are going to help out with your family's business. You are not allowed to see Cindy after tonight."

I was shaking. "I cannot do that. I will never lie, or mislead, or promise a child if I cannot live up to his or her expectations."

"Carol, you have ninety seconds to answer me."

I was sobbing so much that I got up from the chair and walked right out of his office. I called my sister and my friend, who called my therapist, who then called me in for an emergency meeting. It's so funny, my sister was crying because I was crying, and then we had my therapist crying.

I tell you, this was a wicked blow straight to the groin. I felt betrayed, lied to, used, and tossed aside like dirty laundry. I remember while on my way to the therapist, Connor called me on my phone. It went straight to Bluetooth in the new car Connor supposedly bought for me with all the bells and whistles after the divorce.

"Where are you, Carol?"

"I'm on my way to the doctor."

"So you are leaving me alone to tell this lie? It's better if it comes from you because I'm going to have a crying kid on my hands tonight."

"I'm sorry. My head is pounding. My sister left work to be with me. I'm sick about this."

"Carol, I will take care of you. You never have to work. I'll take care of you for as long as you want."

"And I thank you for that. I have to see my doctor to put some sense into this madness. I'm sure we can come to some kind of solution. We need to think about this. Down the road, five, ten, or fifteen years from now, I don't want this day to follow me with guilt."

"Okay, Carol. Talk to you later."

"Okay bye."

I had no contact with Connor that night. Saturday morning, Sharon picked Cindy up from her father's house. Later on Connor called me. "How are you doing?"

"I had better days. I'm not doing well at all."

"How was your celebration party?"

"Not good at all."

"Hmmm. Did you think it would've been happy? Of course not, Connor. It's like telling her I'm dead."

"Can you come to my house at 9:30 a.m. tomorrow?"

"Sure. See you in the morning."

The thing that boggled my mind was that Sharon was not a good mother from day one, and Connor, who was busy making money, paid little attention to Cindy, and the person who was always there for her, even on off days, was treated with such disrespect. I was so involved with her life that Cindy slept over at my apartment. She had toys, her own bed, shampoo, conditioner, a toothbrush, children's Tylenol, stuffed animals, and her favorite blanket at my place. So what the hell was he thinking? Was he that insensitive and cold? I felt so betrayed by both parents. And the thing was they are highly educated people with no common sense.

However, what was in the dark will come to the light one day. Telling a lie will follow with another just to cover the first lie.

That night, my head was pounding so much, so I sat in the dark in my living room just weeping streams of tears thinking I made a promise to a child, and I am not allowed to fulfill it. I am sad and angry at the same time. I got up took two Advil and went to bed .

The next morning, I went over to Connor's house and packed his luggage. He wanted me to drive him to JFK airport. He was going away for the week. I made him sandwiches and packed snacks because some airlines don't offer food. While on the way to the airport, Connor started talking to me, saying he loves me, and he's upset with the ex-wife for putting this kind of pressure on all of us, especially his child.

I said, "Thank you for what you said you were going to do for me."

"Not a problem. You had my back, and all I want is for you to be happy."

"I don't know what to say more than thank you."

We reached the airport. I helped him with his luggage. I was going back in the car when he said, "Wait! Give me a hug and don't cry. Oh, and you'll have to return the new car I bought so that Cindy will think that you are gone, and this week, while I'm out of town, I want you to go find another car, and I'll bill it to my company. Okay. Now smile. Pick me up at the airport on Friday 7:00 a.m., okay?"

"Yes, sure! Thank you. Have a good trip."

"Go have fun. Go car shopping."

I was depressed, but a little happy. Another car? Six months apart. Wow!

The guy was loaded after all. He's a multimillionaire. What I was thinking was that it's not the first car he bought me. Two months after working for him, he bought me a Volvo, so this should be easy. He said, "I'll take care of you. Trust me, Carol."

CHAPTER THIRTEEN

Trust

I TOLD CONNOR I do not trust adults, but I would take my chance with him because he was a man of his word. He told me that the week he was away, he wanted me to make a large grocery for the house and to make a list of all the things to do and fix around the house. After Sharon moved out of the house, I became his personal assistant. I was Jane of all trades. I multi- task, that's what makes me unique.

I went car shopping and could not seem to find a car that would suit me, so I called up a friend who has a friend selling Mercedes Benz. After all, he gave me a promotion a month ago before he told me he's retiring me, so time to upgrade. I wanted to retire in style and comfort. I got the pricing and test drove a 350 ML SUV Mercedes Benz. It was very nice and over $68,000.00. Oh, boy! I don't think he was going for that. I said to myself, *I won't even bother to tell him about that Benz*, so I decided to check out a pre-owned 350RX Lexus with low mileage. It was $35,000.00. Not bad. I made a deposit, and I told the salesman I'd be back in a couple of days to complete the transaction. I texted Connor about the car, and he said okay.

So a couple of days went by, and Connor's vacation ended. I had to pick him up at Kennedy airport. After picking him up, we drove to his office. He asked me to pick him up at 3:30 p.m. I said, "Okay. See you soon."

When I picked him up, he seemed calm. Then I showed him the invoice for the pre-owned Lexus 350 RX. He looked at it, and to my amazement, Connor almost hit the roof.

"$35,000.00 for a car? How are you going to pay for this car? It's too expensive. You'll have to find another job. I can't take care of you for all your life."

"I am stunned and shocked by your reaction, Connor. You told me to go car shopping. You want me to be happy. 'I'll take care of you, and I'll never leave you out in the cold,' you told me."

"And you left a deposit! Go get your money back and go find some other gig!"

"What! I can't believe what you are telling me. My head is so messed up right now. Taking care of kids is the last thing on my mind right now."

"Well, then go on a vacation. Go see your grandkids. $35,000.00 on a car! The first car didn't even cost that much!"

"Well, you told me that I don't have to go job hunting. You also told me that I will not be taking care of kids any more. I am totally confused."

In the past, I saw how he would lie and try to change his stories around, so little did he know every time he wanted to have a meeting with me, I started recording our conversations.

"You must have mistaken what I said to you. You and I will finish this discussion on Saturday."

Saturday came and I didn't call him and he didn't call me either. I was supposed to go to the office to pick up my check, but I decided to stay away from that atmosphere. It was too tense and stressful.

Sunday morning Connor called me.

"Hello," I said in a low tone.

"Hi, how are you?"

"I had better days."

"I miss you. I just wanted to know how you were doing."

"Not good."

"Why don't you go on a vacation? I tried to hire someone to replace you, but it didn't work out. Why don't you come over and cook for me? But you don't have to if you're not up to it. And, go to CVS and pick up my prescription."

"Connor, I don't know what my function is currently with you. I'm clueless. You need to let me know."

"Come over to the house. I'm going to play softball. Come whenever you want."

"Okay bye."

I thought about it over and over, and I decided not to go. Besides, it was Sunday, and I'm not anybody's fucking robot. Come here. Go there. Do this. I was tired of the lies, humiliation, and games. I never felt so much pain, stress, disappointment, deceitfulness, as I felt right then.

I realized now he was trying to cover his own behind. I left my home in Brooklyn and moved to another state to work for these people. I got an apartment in the suburbs, then he begged me to give that up to move into his house to help him get custody of Cindy. Then he gave me two-week notice to move out of his house so that the divorce could settle. Now that it was settled, he kicked me to the curb. All these broken promises and disappointments and to top it off, he tells me, "Look me in the eyes. Trust me." That's what the wolf told Little Red Riding Hood.

The Monday after he came back from his trip, I went to his office to take a package he forgot in the car. He asked me to sit in his office because he wanted to speak with me.

"Okay."

He walked in a few minutes later.

"So how are you?" he asked.

"Not good."

"Look, I don't want you to worry and cry. I won't leave you in the cold. I'll take care of you."

"For how long?"

"For six or seven years."

"So last Friday, it was for as long as I wanted, and now this week, it dropped to six or seven years. Okay."

"I cannot take care of you forever."

"And I know that."

"Okay, then I want you to treat today as a normal work day. Go to the house and take care of business and cook dinner for two days."

"Okay. Is that all?"

"Yes. Put a smile on your face. Don't look so sad."

"Okay. Talk to you later."

I left the office and prepared the meals and left.

Connor has a very powerful voice, and whenever he speaks, everyone just zips it. Sometimes you can't even get half a sentence in. He would say "stop" with authority. It made me feel frustrated at times.

Later in the week, he texted me at 11:20 p.m. "Come in the morning. I will have breakfast with you, and we'll have a talk."

I arrived at 8:00 a.m., fixed breakfast, and he came downstairs.

"How are you?" he asked.

"Not good."

"I want you to lease a car, and I'll bill it to the company."

"Here we go again!"

Connor sighed in frustration.

"All you are doing is hurting my feelings. This is very stressful for me. What I've noticed so far about you and your ex-wife is that you two give then take away. She gave me an $11,000 dollars sofa, and six months later, she came with a truck and repo it. You gave me a car and that too you want to repo. You allowed your child to bond with me, and you ripped her away without a truthful explanation. Now, you are making promises and not keeping them. You are flip flopping on me on a daily basis." By then I was in tears.

"I've been loyal, honest, punctual, reliable, and bent over backwards to facilitate you and your family. I've gone out of my comfort zone to help you with your divorce. I'm a mess because of this. I've asked you to put this in writing since you began flip flopping. Last week, you said I'll take care of you for as long as you want. This week, you're telling me for six or seven years. What will it be in a couple of days?"

"I will speak to you later. I have a very important phone call, and it will take a while. Please treat today as a normal work day."

He left the room and left me hanging with no response. The man had no compassion. He had become cold and ruthless. Sharon really did a number on him. He used to be one of the nicest persons in the world.

CHAPTER FOURTEEN

Lies and Deception

I DON'T KNOW what to make of all this. He used to be very respectful, caring, and compassionate, but I don't think he respects women or have any kind of trust left for people anymore. Now that he was a free man, he was open market, a man of the night. All are welcome. Thank you, pussy, you serve me well. Not a good lifestyle but to each it's own.

A few days later, Connor asked me to come to work. I arrived, made coffee, and sat down. He came downstairs, poured a cup of coffee, and said to me, "How are you?"

"I could be better."

"You know I'll take care of you, right?"

"Yeah, that's what you said."

"Look, I know the type of person you are. You are not the type to sit down and wait for handouts. I'm sure you'll find a job in two or three months, and what if they have a car for you to drive? Then you will not need me to provide you with a car."

"So what are you telling me now? You're flip flopping again!"

"No, I was just speaking hypothetically."

"Hmm?"

There we go again. He's just fucking with my head.

Sunday night at 9:30, a text came in. Well, what do you know? It was Connor.

"Can you pick up my prescription? I need it now, and can you buy me some ice cream too?"

"Okay see you in a bit." *I just hope he is not going to mess with my head again. Enough is enough!*

"Carol, I miss you. It's been difficult for me to get by without you being here. I want you to know that you are family. A friend of mine in New York maybe needing someone to work for them, and I recommended you. They'll pay you well."

"But I live in the suburbs now, and that's in New York. That's what I got away from, plus the commute will be ridiculous, and it will be double tax."

I really don't know what his problem was. He started going over the whole episode again, and I said to myself, *why me, Lord.* He invited me to come and do a puzzle with him, and I said, "I'll pass on that. I'm going home. Good night."

"Here's your check. I will do right by you. I want you to know that. I want you to take a vacation, and when you come back, try to get yourself another job so that I can be off the hook."

"What do you mean by off the hook?"

"Well, as soon as you find another job, I won't have to pay you."

"Okay. That's fine by me. It may take awhile though. I hope you are aware of that, and besides, I'm seeing a therapist now who doesn't think I'm in the right frame of mind. I'll ask my doctor to give me the okay, and then I'll start looking."

"Okay, that's fine."

In my mind, I said to myself, *Hmmm. Tomorrow he'll say something else and then say I misunderstood what he was saying.*

"Oh, and try to get your own car in the next two weeks."

"Are you paying for it?"

"Yes. By the way, can you come to work tomorrow and pick up my dry cleaning?"

"Are you sure about the car this time?"

"I already said yes. You no longer work for me. You are family."

"Ha! I've heard it all before."

Didn't he just say to come to work tomorrow and pick up his dry cleaning? Was he nuts! What do you call that? Family duties? Hmm! Whatever!

Dear Lord, give me the strength and patience to deal with the things I cannot change.

Months after the divorce, all the family assets, such as paintings, silverware, and furniture had to be split 50-50. Sharon showed up one day with the police and movers and basically raped the house of all the expensive things. She even brought along the electrician, plumber, and the mediator lawyer with her. Connor was stunned at how organized she was. Sharon had pictures of every item in the house. She opened every cupboard and cleared it clean. She even threw out the candy that was in candy dishes. All of the chandeliers and even the chairs we were sitting on we had to evacuate so they could be loaded on the truck.

"This is not 50-50. She is wiping you out," I told Connor.

"I know. She's just one nasty bitch."

I stood in the family room, and Sharon passed me by with a pompous attitude. She pulled out some tissue, blew her nose, and looked to her side then threw the tissue behind her so that I would have to pick it up. My blood was boiling, but Connor warned me to be at my best behavior, so I had to contain myself. I went out by the swimming pool and sat under the umbrella in disbelief. How could one person be so materialistic? She was truly a gold digger.

Connor said, "Carol, at this point, I don't care. The fact that she touched it will remind me of her. She's a fucking gold digger, and I hope she never comes back in this house. And at least, we can have some peace."

"You are right! Those things can be replaced."

"I'm just worried about my daughter and what kind of values Sharon is teaching her."

"Me too. I know this is hard for you but stay strong and take this as a learning experience. No pre-nup. No wedding. Lesson learned."

"That was my biggest mistake. I thought she loved me, but instead, she was in love with my money. Why didn't I see that?"

I knew exactly how he felt. It's a feeling you would never forget. And when you recover, with time, your guard will forever be on alert.

CHAPTER FIFTEEN

Trying Times

I HAD NO idea that I would feel the way I was feeling. I asked Connor how Cindy was doing. And he told me, "She misses you, and she cries at night holding the little pillow you gave her."

You see, I have two grown sons and three beautiful grandchildren who I love dearly, and Cindy felt close to me as well, and not having her around made me feel like the pack was incomplete.

I hoped she didn't think I had broken my promise or failed her. I was fired because her mother forbade me from seeing her. That Friday would never be forgotten.

I remember when Cindy was two years old; she would wake up in the middle of the night dragging her blankie and pillow, and she would place it outside the door of my bedroom. She would lay there and fall asleep. Sometimes, she rolled and kicked the door while she was sleeping, and I would wake up by the noise. I'll jump out of bed and scoop her up and put her back in her bed. Those days I'll cherish in my heart.

I know one day she'll try to find me, and I hope it will not be too late. I wish all the best in life for her.

This whole ordeal has taken a toll on me. I would sit in the dark in my apartment and think of Cindy, and I hurt because I know she was hurting. It's the feeling of losing a loved one, not knowing when you'll ever see them again.

I am saddened when I hear certain songs on the radio, such as *When Will I See You Again* and a few others which trigger tears to come. My head was hurting all the time, and I had trouble sleeping, and all I could think was, *I hope she is not going through the heartache that I'm going through.*

Lucky for me, I have my wonderful family who I am very close to. My sister, who is my confidant, and my friend, who would check up on me all the time. I also had my therapist to help me get through the rough times. I saw her every Wednesday. She made me feel better about myself. She's a very nice doctor. She understands and gets it.

I woke up one morning and can't believe I just got a text from Connor telling me I should have been at work at 8:30. What? Really? I thought he said he had to let me go, but now he was texting me to come to work.

I could not understand the mind games. He holds back my rent money and paid it directly to my landlord. I asked him on many occasions to add my rent money to my check, but he refused. He said, "What's the difference? It gets paid anyway." But now that we have a different arrangement, I wanted to cut all ties. I've asked him for my severance pay, but that too was an issue. He would tell me okay, but then he would shun me and continued to call me whenever he wanted errands done. I guess that's what family was all about.

My therapist believed he was controlling and played on people's mind like a chess game. I totally agreed.

I got a phone call from Connor's mother, Roberta. She was crying on the phone and telling me, "You are the best thing that ever happened to Connor besides Cindy."

Connor told her to keep out of his affairs and to do less talking on the phone with me.

Roberta said, "Carol, you are my friend and fuck him. I'll call you whenever I want, and you can call me whenever you want because he is nuts! Stop the lawsuit and stay away from Sharon. She's poison."

"Roberta, what do I have to lose now? I've already lost Cindy and my job. Your son told you to do less talking on the phone with me. Even if I lose my case, my conscious will be cleared."

"Okay. Take care of yourself. I love you. Stay strong."

"Love you too."

I got an email from Connor. "I can't seem to find someone normal to manage the house. Can you come tomorrow night after Cindy goes to her mother's? If not, on Monday morning. Not as someone who worked for me but as a friend to help me out a little."

I emailed him back. "See you on Monday. I am also returning your Jeep." Since he wouldn't buy me the Lexus, I decided to buy something cheaper. I purchased a car with 8,000 miles fairly new SUV. Not bad for $27,000 Let's see if he'll keep his promise and reimburse me.

CHAPTER SIXTEEN

Deceived

ONE MORNING, CONNOR asked me to come to work. I arrived at 8:00 a.m. Connor was upstairs, so I texted him, letting him know that I was downstairs. He texted me saying, "Make me eggs, please."

Connor knew that I wanted help on the down payments for my new car, yet he refused to discuss it.

I would ask him, "Are you going to help me?"

"Sure," he'd say. But I knew he was just beating around the bush and messing with me mentally.

I even told him I was getting a ride with the car salesman. Imagine, I was in his house, and he won't come out of his room because he was avoiding me.

A few minutes later he texted me, *I'm trading and can't talk at the moment. Stop by the office later.*

I drained my bank account to pay for the car because Connor told me not to worry about money, and so I thought why not? I went to the car dealership and got the car. I was so excited. I headed straight to Connor's office. I felt good because he had texted me, asking me how much money I needed. I reached his office, and Connor asked me to wait in his office for a few minutes. I sat down, and two minutes later, he walked in and shut the door.

"How much money did you pay down?"

"$6,000.00."

"What? Why the hell did you do that?"

"Because you told me not to worry about money, and the more I put down, the quicker I finish paying for the car."

"That makes no sense to me! Why would you drain your bank account to pay down on a car?"

"Because you said to trust you!!"

The room got silent for about two minutes, and then I said, "I feel like I'm becoming a burden to you. Do you think I like asking you for money. Why don't you just give me my severance package and let me go. Why are you controlling my rent and controlling my life? I asked you if you were going to fire me, and you said 'yes and no.' Make up your mind, please. This is stressing me out."

I saw my therapist. I left her office feeling good, and now after meeting with Connor, I felt like one foot was forward and the other was ten feet back. He always left me feeling nervous and hanging.

Later that night, Connor called me.

"Tell me I'm the greatest."

"Why?"

"Tell me I'm the greatest."

"Do I have my job back?"

"No, you don't. That's a done deal. I found you a job."

"Where?"

"I found you a job in New York City."

"But I live in New Jersey now, and the commute will be ridiculous. Plus, I'll have to pay double tax."

"Well, you can move back to Brooklyn. I gave these people your phone number, and they'll call you."

"Okay. We'll see how that goes."

"Have a good night."

"You too."

Who the fuck does he think he is? He said he would take care of me and I'll never have to worry about money, and now, when it was time to help with the car, it's excuse, excuse, one after another. And now he was job hunting for me.

Then all of a sudden, I got a text from Roberta.

"How are you? Can't wait to see you and hug you. Connor needs you. He just doesn't realize how much just yet. I'm flying in a week or so. Love you. See you soon."

"Love you too. See you soon."

This situation was a nightmare. I felt like I was in a bad dream. Roberta did not have any clue of what was going on. Connor didn't want his family to know everything that was happening. He wanted them out of his affairs.

I had to take my therapist advice very seriously. I needed to put an end to this so that I could move on with my life. Easier said than done.

Right now, I felt like the job that I loved doing for decades had come to a halt. I felt that my image had been tarnished. My passion stolen. I was depressed. I didn't feel like being around people or friends with kids. I was just sad and felt like I was in mourning. I missed Cindy so much it was unimaginable. Now, when I look back, the same thing that Sharon did to Connor, he was doing back to me. Maybe he wanted someone to share his pain. But why me?

He begged me to give up my apartment and give away my furniture because there was no point in putting it in storage; then he gave me two weeks to move out of his house—all the while promising to reimburse me, which he never did. When I confronted him to reimburse me, he said, "That's a part of life." So $28,000 later out of my savings and now he was balling around and fucking with my head. His words, "Don't worry, I got your back. Look me in the eye. I'll never leave you in the cold" had no fucking merit. They were all lies, lies, and more fucking lies.

I cannot stand grown people looking you in the face and insulting your intelligence. Connor thought he's the smartest person in the world. He thought he was one step ahead of everyone else and treated everyone else as a chess game. I felt like I was in captivity and needed to escape. It was hard because I was close to his family, which was another story. His family had health issues, and this would only cause more pain and stress.

Right now, I felt deceived by him. I had to do right by me now and take charge of my life. This was not healthy. I was so depressed I didn't feel like leaving the house. I felt as though if I took care of one more child I would go into serious depression. I promised Cindy that I would not take care of anymore kids, and now Connor was trying to make me a liar by finding me a job to take care of a child in New York and go back to the train rides to reunite with my 600 train friends in the concrete jungle with noisy neighbors, loud sirens, gunshots, and take a step down and start over again. Was he out of his fucking mind? I was sad and angry at the same time. I felt mentally abused and taken advantage of by both Sharon and Connor.

I decided to speak to Connor one more time to give him a chance to redeem himself. If that didn't work, then I'll have to do what was best for me.

In the meantime, I got all my receipts and expenditures ready for a labor department attorney because this was getting fucking ridiculous. This is the twenty first century, and I was going to exercise my rights as an American citizen. Most employers only like what you can do for them, using the words, "I love you," when they want something from you.

Fuck that shit! Those are the most overrated and misused words in the world used by adults. Nothing is for free. I am aware of that. I could do without the flattering and show me the love on my paycheck. Hey, that works well.

Connor never let anyone get too close to him. Anytime you got too close, he would separate himself from you. Nothing you do for him was good enough, and whenever he made a mistake, he blamed everyone but himself.

Well, I had enough of that shit. It was now my time to shine and get pass this because at the end of the day it was just a job. My problem was that I got my emotions wrapped up with this family who I happened to love. In the future, I had to do things differently by not opening my heart to anyone.

CHAPTER SEVENTEEN

Intervention

EVEN THOUGH I was trying hard to put all this drama behind me and move on with my life, it was very difficult. I found myself waking up around 2:00 a.m. each day, and who do I call—my sister Monique. She never complained. She cried because I cried. She shared my grief and pain. I love her for her patience.

Well, Monique couldn't take the pressure that was building up, and unknowing to me, she called Connor and left a message for him on his service. Later, she told me of their conversation.

"Connor, hi Monique here. What are you doing to my sister? Call me when you can."

"Hi, Monique. I'm not doing anything wrong. I'm a good man. I spent a lot of money trying to save Carol's job, and I lost. My ex is suing me, and it's because Carol is suing her."

"And you told her to sue your ex. Listen, Connor, I know everything that's going on."

"No you don't. You stop! And listen to me."

"No! You stop! Stop stringing Carol along. You fired her! And you are still asking her to come to work. What kind of a sick joke is that? When you fire someone, you don't ask them to return to work. I heard you on the car's Bluetooth while on the way to see her therapist. You said you would take care of Carol for six to seven years or how long it takes. Well, cut the crap and make a clean break.

Do the right thing if it's your decision to take care of her for the time you said. Or, why not pay her off and let her go instead of controlling her living arrangements. It's not healthy for her. The surrounding has too much bad memories. She needs to move on."

"What can I do to make her happy?"

"Were you not listening to me? You are a wealthy man, and everything you gave my sister, you reposed. I feel sick to my stomach that you can treat another human being the way you treated my sister. She had your back, drained her bank account, made her give up her apartment, and gave up her furniture to have her move into your home to help you then give her two weeks to move out after she helped you and six months later you fired her! Are you kidding me? All because you are scared of Sharon filing for full custody? Wear the pants in your house! Who's advising you?"

"The professionals are."

"So the professionals told you to lie to Cindy?"

"Yes."

"Well, those professionals need to find another profession. So that's why you told your daughter that Carol left the country, and you don't know when she'll return? Shame on you! Bad, bad moral ethics. Connor, one thing in life is never lie to your child. She will not remain small. She'll grow up, and you'll have to cover that lie and another and another, and eventually, her whole life will be a lie. Cindy will not trust both you or Sharon, and she'll end up hating her parents and have trust issues. Now, you think about that."

"I'm not stringing her along. Carol is getting bad advice."

"You recommended those lawyers to Carol, and you told my sister you want her to crush Sharon with the lawsuit. You paid for the retainer fee, so what are you saying?"

Connor was silent.

"You told her that you are not going to leave her without a car, and up to this day not one damn cent you paid. Carol had to drain her bank account to buy a car. Is that how you thank people? That's the most ungrateful thing you can do to anyone. I hope you can look yourself in the mirror. What goes around comes around. Now, you think about that. You and your ex have offended me and my family."

"What can I say? That's a part of life."

"Is that all you can say?"

"I'm a good man, Monique. You'll see."

"Yeah right! Goodbye."

"Have a good one."

I was relaxing at home when my phone rang. It was Monique.

"Hi, dear sis. How are you?"

"I just got off the phone with Connor, and I'm fucking pissed. That motherfucker is so cold. My blood is boiling."

"Oh, Oh! What the hell happened to you two?"

"I just told him what I thought. Are you okay? I worry about you. Of all the people in the world, why you? You are the kindest, honest, reliable, sweetest person that ever lived on this planet. This is not fair. That man is so cold and ruthless. He used you and kicked you to the curb."

I began crying. I couldn't help myself. The stress and pain was too much. I needed some kind of release or I might explode.

"Oh, please don't cry, Carol. This too will pass, and you'll look back at this and wonder why you stressed this. Time heals all wounds. Maybe you should go away on a vacation. A change of scenery would help. Remember, you have family members that love you very much. Your children love you. Your grandkids love you. Think positive thoughts."

CHAPTER EIGHTEEN

Sacrifice

I HAVE ALWAYS had trust issues in the past, but now I'm scarred for life. When someone tells you, "Look me in the eye. Listen to me. Do you hear me? Trust me. I will take care of you. You never have to look for another job. I will never leave you in the cold," and then two weeks later, he fires you, and then go job hunting for you, it is hard not to be frightened. How can I ever trust anyone again?

My main reason for standing up for Connor was because I didn't want Cindy to grow up without her father, and I knew it was a risk I had to make. This situation was outside my comfort zone, having to blow the whistle on Sharon. But, after all the begging and pleading from Connor, I felt compelled to do the right thing. Sometimes you have to wonder if you should help some people. All I did was tell the truth, and the truth got me in trouble. But then again, it was fundamental for Cindy to have both parents in her life. No child should be deprived of that.

I had both my parents in my life growing up, and my parents were separated due to the death of my dad. Divorce was something I wasn't use to as a child or teenager. Besides, when average people get divorced, they never go through all this madness. But, money changes everything. When average people get a divorce, you can't wait to throw his or her sorry ass out the door or to leave with no forwarding address. It was so sad that Sharon was using Cindy as a pawn, a trade, a weapon in order to suck as much money out of Connor. She was sacrificing her child's mental stability and moral values for the love of money and greed.

I sent an email to Connor. I asked him to bring my mail to the office. He emailed me back saying, "It's only junk mail." Then added, "I spoke to Monique. We had a long talk. She's awesome. I don't want you to be sad, and I'm here to help you if you want."

Ha! He's not going to wheel me in with that smooth talk. My heart had become hardened toward people who tell lies. Connor was a good and loyal man, but his experience with Sharon had destroyed a part of his goodness and moral values.

Sharon was so furious with me at blowing the whistle on her that she made part of the agreement in the divorce to limit my contact with Cindy, and none of my friends or family members should be hired to replace me. That made me furious that she would come up with that shit, discriminating me, my family, and my friends. So, in other words, if I lied and agreed to Sharon's demands, I would be fine, but if I told the truth, I would be screwed. I'm sorry but fuck that shit! I'm not telling lies for no one. I'm very fearful of God. People can fool other people, but God is always watching. That is what I was brought up to believe. My mother told me, "When you do bad, bad will follow you, and you will be destined for hell." That always rings in the back of my head.

Connor said he thought once Sharon got her lump sum of cash, she would leave me alone because she was aware of how close Cindy was with me. Boy, was he wrong. That bitch came back with a vengeance to destroy. Sharon filed papers with the court for Connor to give her a life insurance of one million dollars for Cindy of which Sharon wanted to be the beneficiary. And she also wanted him to pay for more legal fees. Ain't that a bitch. When was this madness ever going to stop?

CHAPTER NINETEEN

Lawsuit

I SUED SHARON for discriminating my family, friends, and me—for coaching me to commit perjury in court during litigation of her divorce from Connor and for mental anguish, stress, and punitive damages. Connor encouraged me to sue Sharon. He even paid the lawyer's retainer fees. He also introduced me to someone to guide me through the process but insisted that I did not mention his name. I guess that was his way of getting back at Sharon for getting half his cash and properties.

Now, I felt so intertwined, hoping this would end sooner than later. The court system is so damn slow. I don't wish this situation on my worst enemy. It was hell. I couldn't leave my apartment without being followed by people with binoculars and cameras. I was followed by strange people, as though I were a criminal. Holy shit! I'm popular in the worst way.

I've made a couple of police reports, but the police said they couldn't do anything because no crime was committed. I felt tortured, stressed, and violated, and all of a sudden, the American Dream was slowly crumbling before me. Thank God my children are adults. Could you imagine having to go through this with small children?

Lawsuits were now Sharon's hobby. Anything to make Connor's life miserable was her main goal. After all, she made it quite clear to Connor and myself that she would make his life a living hell. The word civil was not in Sharon's vocabulary toward anyone that triggered her anger.

One day, while running my regular errands, I saw this Ford Edge SUV following me. I decided to turn into different streets to try and lose the person following me but with no success. Everywhere I went, that SUV was on my trail. I decided to go to the library, and what do you know—there's that SUV. It was a woman with a camera taking pictures of me and my vehicle. This was fucking ridiculous now.

I got out of my vehicle, and the woman took my photograph. I approached the woman, who by now was smoking a cigarette. Trying to be calm, I approached her with caution because I didn't know if she was carrying a weapon and said, "Why are you following me, and what's up with taking my photo?"

She said, "No reason!"

"Please leave me alone." Then I went into the library and looked out through the window. She was out there walking around my car, and then she went into her SUV and sped off. I came out of the library and noticed the valve for my car tires were missing, and the car was off balanced.

I knew then and there that it was the work of Sharon. Her old stalking ways resurfaced, and now I was the target. I can't count how many people Sharon sued in the past. Sharon sued almost all the decorators, contractors, or anyone who had a big contract to work with her. No one had sued her before. By suing her, I was giving her a dose of her own medicine, and it seemed like she couldn't handle it.

Sharon pissed me off that time with the tissue incident. It was one of the most belittling things you can do to a person. It's like spitting on someone, and the only thing that came to mind was racism and discrimination and slavery. You would think in this day and age we've overcome this type of behavior. Some people pretend that this is not an issue, but when someone gets angry, the issue will resurface, and you get flashbacks of segregation and what our human rights leaders fought for. If I let this pass, then the great Dr. Martin Luther King Jr. would have died in vain.

Sharon needed to be put in her place, and she knew I would not stand for this bullshit. The lawsuit would be pursued. Now, I did not care if I didn't collect punitive damages, but the world needed to know of her wrongdoings and unlawful acts against a child and other human beings.

CHAPTER TWENTY

Tense Moments

ONE MONTH LATER, Roberta called me.

"Carol, I miss you so much. Nothing is the same anymore at Connor's house. The love and warmth has disappeared, and all that's left is coldness. Connor is doing a lot of different activities with Cindy to keep her occupied, but Cindy has her moments when she won't interact with anyone."

They all went to a family event where all the families got together, a very chilling moment for both Connor and Sharon's family. Of course, Sharon came with Charlie the dog. Cindy wanted her cousin, the son of Jessica who is Connor's sister, to come over and pet Charlie. Jessica decided to accompany her son to pet Charlie. Sharon was sitting there, less than a foot away, and to Jessica's surprise, Sharon started to weep, and suddenly she got up and hugged Jessica, telling her she missed the family and it had been difficult for her dealing with the divorce.

Jessica stepped back and said, "Sharon, it didn't have to end like this. You're not a nice person, and what you did to my family will never be forgotten."

Sharon traded that loving family and used Cindy as a pawn and recently to file another lawsuit against Connor, so all those crocodile tears were not fooling anybody. Connor's family didn't trust her anymore. She was too trifling, so much so that Roberta refused to have anything to do with Sharon. Could you blame her?

One week later, Connor's secretary called me to give me the heads up that Connor refused to sign my paychecks. His excuse was he had to show a financial statement and did not want to have checks pending. That was such a petty excuse for a multimillionaire, who, I know for a fact, does not have financial problems.

I sent him an email, and his reply was, "I'm not stopping your pay FYI."

Later on that same day, Connor called me on my phone, "Carol, not to worry. I'm going to pay you."

"When?"

"Oh, not to worry about that. You'll get a check soon."

I sent him another email to meet with him at his office, and he agreed to see me in two days.

This was his last chance to come clean and stop lying and misleading me. Every one of the recordings I did on Connor, he changed his story. It was very frustrating to listen to a compulsive liar.

I got another email from Connor postponing our meeting. I changed my doctor's appointment to facilitate the time he wanted me to come by. That was fine by me. No sooner before I left my house, I checked my email, and he sent another one to postpone again. This was fucking ridiculous. He's been stepping on my toes for too long, and I would love to cut all ties with him, but I was still friends with Roberta, and she expressed how much she appreciated my friendship. Before all this craziness began, Roberta became very ill and had to be on chemotherapy. She stayed at Connor's home, and I took care of her. She was always grateful toward me, so turning my back on her was unimaginable. I loved talking to her.

But Connor needed to man up and keep his agreements and promises. He asked me to come to his office, and upon my arrival, he smiled at me and said, "How are you and how's your health," as though there was no bad blood between us.

"Well, since you asked I'll tell you. Hypertension, depression, anxiety attacks, insomnia, side effects from the medicine, and extreme emotional stress."

"Well, Carol, I know you to be a very hardworking and confident person, but it's obvious you are a mess. You need to find work and move on. If you drop the lawsuit, I'll allow you to see Cindy, but you must continue to lie to her. If you can promise me that you'll tell her that you went to the Caribbean to take care of your mom and worked in your family's restaurant, then I'll set up a meeting for you. If you can do that for me, then I'll be generous to you and give you a big check to take care of you for the rest of the year." Now, this is the end of June. Connor wrote a check for seventy-six hundred dollars. To sum it up, it's six weeks pay, and to add insult to injury, in the memo, he wrote, "final paycheck." He got up, bent over, hugged me, and said, "I love you. You are like family."

"Really? You're math is way off."

"No! No! I'm being nice and very generous to you, Carol." Connor placed the check on his desk. "Take it."

"Connor, you asked me to give up my apartment twice."

"I know that, Carol. Take the check and put a smile on your face."

This was a damn nightmare. I can't believe this was the same person who told me to trust him. He promised to reimburse me for all the moving expenses. I stormed out of his office, leaving the check on his desk. I never touched it.

When his behind was in heat with the custody battle, Connor and his family begged me not to leave, and in return, Connor promised to take care of me. I gave him enough chances to redeem himself. I don't know what the hell he was thinking. Clearly he forgot his ex-wife asked me to tell a lie, and I refused. I'll keep my pride and dignity, so thank you very much.

The next week, I relieved my lawyer of his duties with the lawsuit against Sharon, and I hired a well-known law firm for a double lawsuit against Sharon and Connor. Sorry Roberta and to the rest of your family, but your son is not a man of his word. He lies, and he's not the man he made me to believe in.

In the back of my mind, I remembered how he tricked dozens of women who came to the house at least four times a week. During and after his divorce, Connor used his mansion and sophisticated cars as a pussy trap. He had become so ruthless and careless. He would contact them through Internet dating services and through friends who would hook him up. Each night, there was a different female. When she arrived, they head straight to his master bedroom. His bedroom had a scary look to it, and it was accentuated by a huge piece of artwork over the bed that looked like blood red dripping paint.

If he liked the date, he would put on a sexy movie. But if he was disappointed with the date, he would put on a scary, crime drama movie called Dexter. The next day, he bragged about how well the movie scared his date away.

It was so disgusting how he behaved. And when these women left their items behind, he would have me place them in a bag and label the dates name on it. Many times, he confused the bags and gave it to the wrong owner. When this occurred, he would then claim them to be his sister's belongings.

Those women could not resist his wealth. What can I say? He loved his gold diggers. Some of them would bring drugs and sex toys. I could hear moaning from these women all the way down the hall. And to top it all off, most of these women were in professional fields. They were lawyers, doctors, nurses, interior decorators, and from many other professions, so you would think they would know better than to carry on in this manner of having one night stands.

Lying had become an important part of Connor's lifestyle. The lies got so bad that he would even text or email me to confirm a lie for him. He should know better. I don't condone lies. Lying to those women was bad, but they are gold diggers and are consenting adults.

When Connor started telling me to lie to Cindy, I realized he had lost his mind. He lied to his business partners, his family, his friends, all the women who came to the house. I just didn't go for that shit. Besides, I was just the nanny.

My attorney suggested that we send Connor a letter of demand to settle peacefully. Connor responded to my attorney telling him he'll resolve the situation and agreed to meet with him, but he must come alone. My attorney agreed. Imagine, Connor tried to bamboozle my attorney, digging a deeper ditch for himself. My attorney said it didn't matter what Connor says. My recordings speak for itself. Now, everyone will know what a jerk he was. Connor took my kindness for weakness.

There are times when I didn't feel like leaving my apartment. I felt like I was being watched. I was recently followed by another vehicle. I was not paranoid. Court documents proved that I was under surveillance by Sharon. The length that wealthy people do to get their way is absurd and ridiculous. The more money they have, the crazier they are.

CHAPTER TWENTY-ONE

Carol Now

MONTHS HAVE PASSED, and my lifestyle started to change. The things I like to do seemed not too important these days. I continue to see my therapist and my doctor, who prescribed antidepressants and sleeping pills for me. I had to give up my apartment and sell some of my jewelry to keep up with everyday needs. I moved in with a family member, who offered to help. I started doing casual work so as to stretch my savings. Life is tough, and I'm struggling, but I'm holding my head above waters. I keep singing the song *I Will Survive*.

It is so ironic. I got an email the other day from Connor wishing me a happy birthday. I did not respond. Connor's sister texted me to also wish me a happy birthday, and I did not respond either. My attorney advised me to cut all ties with that family.

Finally, the depositions have begun, and Connor was the first to be served. The deposition took place at his attorney's office. I must say, Connor spoke very highly of me. But insisted that he never made any promises to me, and we had no contract. Again, he was lying, but, this time, under oath. Why was I not surprised? It was a normal way of life for him.

My attorney asked him, "Do you think Carol's termination was justified?"

Connor's attorney objected to the question.

I looked Connor straight in the eyes, and Connor mumbled to his attorney saying, "I want to answer."

His lawyer asked for a break to confide with him.

Connor came back in the room saying he wished to continue. And my attorney repeated the question. Connor answered, no. My attorney asked him if he understood the question, and Connor said, "If it wasn't for my ex-wife, Carol would still be working for me."

When the deposition was over, Connor reached out and shook hands with my attorney and me and said, "How's the lawsuit with Sharon coming along?"

I was stunned. Shouldn't he be worried about his own lawsuit? I just shrugged my shoulders and said, "It's coming along."

Next was Sharon's deposition. I had gotten caught up in a traffic jam and reached late. Everyone was sitting in the conference room of Sharon's attorney. All eyes turned to me. Sharon's persona changed as I walked in the room. I could feel the coldness and hostility radiating out of her. I sat down. My attorney advised me not to worry. "We were waiting for you, and besides, he, too, arrived late."

Sharon started making up lies as she went along. Most of the questions her attorney objected. So my lawyer said, "There is no point to continue my line of questions since you are objecting most of them."

So my lawyer filed a motion for all their divorce documents. And, of course, they filed a motion to argue. In the end, all records were awarded to my lawyer. Now, he filed a motion for a trial date and a jury of six people and a motion to consolidate both lawsuits. I know there is cause for concern on Sharon's part because the ruling by the court is presently on the Internet.

It has been seventeen months since I last saw Cindy. I always wonder if or when will I see her again.

One evening, I was sitting home with my family when I got a text. It was Connor's sister. *My daddy just died of pancreatic cancer. It has been a horrible ordeal for all of us. We miss you. XOXO. P.S. I posted on Facebook. I'm having a Shiva at my home, and you are invited.*

I haven't texted or spoken to that family for over a year, and now this!

After speaking to my family I decided to text her. *OMG! Please accept my condolences to you and your family.*

And there started the reconnections. Connor's sister replied. She understood the situation and did not hold any animosity against me. She loved me and missed me a lot. I texted her saying, *This weighs heavily on me. I would like to come but don't want to be rejected twice.*

She reassured me that the situation with Connor and Sharon had nothing to do with how they felt about me. I texted her, "How is Roberta doing? How is she holding up?"

She replied, "Okay."

I texted Roberta. "Please accept my condolences. I'm very sorry for your loss. Please be strong. My thoughts and prayers are with you. I would like to be there, but I don't want to be rejected twice. Always thinking of you."

Roberta replied, "Needed you so much. Your words meant the most. Needed you these past months. We spoke of you often. We both missed you a lot. Love you so much."

"I never stopped thinking of you. Be strong. XOXO."

The funeral took place the following day. I decided to go show my respects to Connery and the rest of the family. Yet I was still skeptical about the situation. After all, Connor was going to be there, and I did not know what his reactions would be. A big lawsuit was in effect, and I could be in a hostile environment.

I arrived at the temple, and it was empty. Was this a hoax? My heart started throbbing, and I was very aware of my surroundings. Suddenly, I saw a man walking toward me dressed in a black suit. I got in my car, locked the doors, and started the ignition, and suddenly, he passed my car and headed to the car parked next to mine. Phew! I lowered my window down and asked him, "Is there a funeral here today?"

"Oh, you mean Connery Goldstein?"

"Yes."

"Oh, that funeral was at twelve noon and lasted only an hour."

"Thank you, sir, but who are you?"

"I'm the funeral director."

"Thank you very much, sir."

No wonder there was nobody here. I was two hours late.

My next stop was at Jessica's house for the Jewish Shiva, which was twenty minutes away. I headed over to Jessica's house. I arrived and sat in my car, and after five minutes or so, I saw a fleet of black limos driving toward the private road to Jessica's home. The first limo stopped, and Connor came out of the car followed by Roberta, Jessica, Joslyn, and a few other family members.

I took a deep breath preparing myself for whatever would happen and got out of the car. Roberta saw me and walked straight toward me with open arms. We hugged and cried together with her head pulled back, so she could look at me, maybe to see if I was real. I wiped her eyes, and she said, "I'm so happy to see you. I needed you so badly. I missed you more than I miss my right hand. I wanted to call you, but I'm afraid of my son. He's controlling. I was stuck in the house for seven months caring for Connery. It was horrible. You are my friend, and I was forced to choose. But now you are here. Fuck it! I love you very much." The hugs and kissed on the cheek continued from Roberta to Jessica and then Joslyn. All the while, Connor looked on to my surprise. Connor walked over to me. My heart was racing. His arms opened, he hugged me, and said, "Thank you for coming. My family and I love you."

I said, "I'm sorry for your loss. I too cared for Connery deeply."

"Oh. Carol. Cindy is here."

I told Connor it was best that I leave before she saw me because Sharon did not want me to have any contact with Cindy.

Connor said, "At this point, I don't give a damn what Sharon wants. The point is that Cindy lost her grandfather, and it's a sad day for her. Seeing you will make a big difference."

"Are you sure?"

"Yes."

Cindy and her cousins were playing in the basement. Connor decided to make a grand entrance. He turned off the lights to the basement, and the kids yelled, "Hey, who did that?"

Connor answered, "It's' me you guys."

One of the kids said, "Hey, Uncle Connor, turn the lights on."

Connor asked, "Cindy, where are you?"

"Here, Daddy."

"Cindy, come to the doorway. I have a very big surprise for you."

"Okay."

"1, 2, 3," Connor counted then switched the lights on.

Cindy looked up with her eyes wide opened in shock when she saw me. She ran to me with arms wide open and hugged and cuddled me with her arms and legs wrapped around me. She was screaming, then said, "Carol, Carol is it really you? I miss you. I miss you. I miss you so much. I never stopped thinking of you. I love you so much. I think of you every day and night."

"I missed you too and love you very much and that will never change."

It was a tearful moment for both of us and after that Cindy started giggling and acting silly. She asked me where I was, and I told her I was away to take care of some business. I was warned by Connor to be careful of what I said to Cindy. After all, I'm not stupid. Cindy's mentality was too fragile at this stage to talk about her parents firing me, which were the real reasons why I could not be around her. I had to keep my indifference with her parents to myself to protect her. After all, they are the ones raising her, and I didn't want Cindy to have anger issues toward them, for it may lead to other problems.

Cindy continued to hug and kiss my cheeks, and I hugged and kissed her on the head.

Cindy then yelled out, "This is the best day of my life."

One of Cindy's cousins said, "How could you say that when we just buried papa."

Cindy said, "Well, I don't know about you, but it's the best day of my life."

Cindy told me that the pictures are still hanging in the corridors, and she told everyone not to remove them. I avoided any questions from Cindy by distracting her about her beautiful blue dress and jewelry and her hair. I asked her about Charlie, and she told me she had another dog.

The whole time we spent together Cindy's arms was around my waist. She was squeezing my waist and shaking me and telling me how much she longed for this day to happen.

This girl was on cloud nine. It was a tearful and emotional reunion—one that may never happen again, unless, when she gets old enough to make her own decisions, and she'll have to find me. I must say that reunions with close friends and family are priceless.

It was such a shame that it took losing a loved one to bring long lost friend together. The reunion brought a little peace and answers to questions that bothered me. I thought that Roberta was mad at me for suing her son, but she knew too that he lied and mislead me and didn't keep his word. Connor's entire family were aware of the agreement that Connor and I agreed to and are all disappointed in him of how this whole situation turned out.

Jessica informed me that Connor told the family the lawsuit had nothing to do with them and not to hold it against me but to hold it against Sharon. He was so bitter toward Sharon. I overheard him telling a couple of people at Jessica's home that Sharon continues to make his life a living hell. She was suing him for legal fees and breach of postdivorce agreements. Those two have become very popular with attorneys and the courthouse.

CHAPTER TWENTY-TWO

Lawsuits

MY LAWSUIT CONTINUED, and I was deposed eight times. Those drilling depositions went on for hours and were very exhausting. The only thing they didn't ask me was how many times I went to the toilet. They asked for bank statements, medical history, check books, W2's for the past seven years, leases, receipts, my passport, emails, text messages, termination letter, my level of education, reasons for coming to the US, and background of my country. It was a nightmare of headaches and a lot of stress.

My second deposition was full of surprises. During our lunch break, Connor rushed out of the conference room. My lawyer and I walked slowly behind him. We sat down in the lobby for a short chat, and to my amazement, Connor came over and asked to speak to my attorney. He told Connor he could speak with me present. Connor said, "WTF are you doing? You didn't prepare Carol properly for this deposition. I want Sharon to pay. I don't want her coming after me."

My attorney said, "I want my client to speak the truth."

Connor was concerned about the discovery of documents that will vindicate him. Connor was clever enough to select the ones that Sharon alone was guilty for the wrongful termination and intentional infliction of emotional stress. I was stressed out. My heart started pounding out of control with numbness and tingling in my body. My blood pressure started rocketing high. I began hyperventilating, feeling confused and feeling claustrophobic. I had to be rushed to the ER to find out that these symptoms were the cause of a severe panic attack. I had to postpone my deposition for the rest of that week and continued the following week. And you would think Sharon's attorneys would have some kind of compassion, but they did not. The morning of the deposition, I gave my attorney a letter from my doctor and the hospital ER's discharge papers. They were pissed off at the restrictions. They wanted to argue against my doctor's recommendations that I get frequent breaks and that I should not be questioned under any kind of pressure for a long period of time. They eventually agreed that they'll try to make the days shorter.

After going through all the depositions, I got a call from my attorney. Sharon's name was not on my W2's, so technically, the person who actually fired me was Connor. That bastard! He claimed it was because of Sharon that he had to let me go. But, according to the court papers, it never said I couldn't see Cindy, and he knew this all along. Oh, the lies with Connor only got worse. He lied under oath saying that he was shocked when he heard I sued Sharon when he was the one who initiated it in the first place. He even gave me the money to retain a lawyer, and he told me he wanted me to sue Sharon for millions of dollars, and he would help me by providing all the evidence needed along with an advisor to navigate and pursue the lawsuit. Connor realized that Sharon found out and he was pissed off at me. Sadly, my lawyers advised me that it was no use going after Sharon because my evidence wasn't strong enough. It was her words against my words. Even though Sharon was the cause and instigator for me being fired, the documents tell otherwise.

I am still disturbed about Sharon encouraging Cindy to sing along with her to that disgusting song, "penis in the butt," during the height of the divorce. That was so disgusting for a mother to be teaching her daughter. I realized, too, that by me bringing this up in the lawsuit, it will expose Sharon, and Connor will have some evidence to file for full custody of Cindy. So again, he was using me long before he fired me. Finally, I withdrew the lawsuit against Sharon but continued to sue Connor.

A couple of days passed, and I received a text from Connor, "I cannot believe you withdrew the lawsuit on Sharon. Your lawyers are stupid. And they don't know what they are doing. You are not the person I thought I knew. You are not protecting my daughter. Your grandson will not be proud of you."

Connor has really lost his mind. WTF does my grandson have to do with this?

In an email from the discovery of documents for the court, Connor signed and agreed with Sharon that I have no contact with Cindy, yet he was pretending he was the good guy. I was not supposed to have contact with Cindy, yet I was supposed to protect her? He is nuts!

I decided to ignore him. He texted me, asking for my sister's phone number. Since that didn't work, he called me on my cell phone begging me to drop the lawsuit against him because it was hurting him. I said to him, "I haven't slept without sleeping pills in two years. I'm on antidepressants. I'm in therapy, and I ended up in the hospital due to extreme emotional stress that you intentionally inflicted on me, and you want me to drop the lawsuit against you! Not in this life. Speak to my lawyers."

I know he started to panic because he started to make a settlement offer. Connor said, "How much can I offer you to drop the lawsuit against me?"

I said, "This is out of my hands. You have to speak to my attorney."

"If you let this case go to trial, you will lose."

"Why is that?"

"Because I have all the trump cards."

"What are you talking about? Do you think this is a card game?"

"I have a strategy to force you to stop, and you'll end up with nothing, and I'm scared that Cindy will find out when she gets older, and I'll look like the bad guy. So, I want to give you a little something for this to stop. Look, I'll give you some Knicks tickets and some fine jewelry from my store. You can sell it and recover a lot of cash."

"Thanks, but no thanks. Speak to my lawyers. You lied and deceived me! Goodbye!"

I emailed my lawyer to let him know about Connor's ridiculous offer.

Now, I realized the cat and mouse game that Connor was playing with everyone. Connor filed a motion to disqualify the law firm who represented me. And he also filed a lawsuit against me, and he also sued the advisor he recommended to help navigate the lawsuit against Sharon.

The lawsuit against Sharon was strictly Connor's idea, but the suit against Connor was one hundred percent me because he lied and mislead me. Everything he said he would do while the lawsuit against Sharon was in progress he turned his back on me. The word "trust me" was a very powerful word with life changing meaning.

Connor had become very ruthless, and by suing the law firm and the advisor, legal fees for everyone's defense was building up. The judge ordered a conference and recommended to the attorneys to speak with their clients to settle. I could hear Connor arguing in the corridor of the court. He was negotiating back and forth. Connor had four counts denied by the court.

CHAPTER TWENTY-THREE

The Settlement

CONNOR AGREED TO drop his lawsuit against me and the law firm, and in return, I agreed to drop three counts and the other count. The judge told Connor he was guilty and needed to pay compensation for lost wages and severance pay. Connor's head remained down the whole time. His attorney spoke on his behalf. I could see the embarrassment on his face. We all signed the agreement, and I walked over to Connor's attorney and said, "Hi, Mr. Robinson. I just wanted you to know that I spoke the whole truth and nothing but the truth. I never fabricated or told a lie about Sharon. She is a sick individual and need help."

Connor's attorney said, "We never doubted you. Connor speaks very well of you."

"I'm sorry it had to come to this, but Connor was given the opportunity to settle our agreement long before we ended up here before a judge.

"Connor cares about you."

"Really! He had a fine way of showing it. Well, I still care about him and his family. Have a good day sir."

We left the court, and one of my attorneys said, "Connor is one deceitful snake who plays with people's minds, and it really gives him an adrenaline rush to win."

The lawsuit between Connor and Sharon continues, but thank God I'm done with that chapter of my life.

Sharon is now suing Connor for additional legal fees, and the mystery continues with those two. As for Cindy, I will always love her. I hope she has a good and happy life. With this experience, I felt tarnished and lost interest in working for people with young children.

As for Connor's family, I understand why we became distant. Blood is thicker than water. This is the end of a ruthless chapter of my life.

This journey is one that I'll never forget—the long work hours for one flat pay, the commitment, the loyalty and honesty that did not pay off, and the long term emotional stress has affected me mentally and physically.

I have no desire to care for other people's children. My therapist advised me to write all my thoughts and feeling down to help cleanse my brain from the nightmare of that toxic environment, so here it is written down and forever put behind me.

CPSIA information can be obtained
at www.ICGtesting.com
Printed in the USA
LVHW09*0350240918
591096LV00007BA/256/P